"You want a coach, you've got a coach,"

Andrea stated. She plucked the highball out of Ian's hand. "But no more alcohol—" she picked up the lit cigarette resting in the ashtray and dropped it into the drink "—and no more smoking. I'll see you in the morning, six o'clock sharp," she said, then turned and walked out of the restaurant.

"Andrea, wait," Ian called, following her.

She swung around to face him.

"You told me I needed a tremendous amount of determination to do this," he said. "I think I have what it takes."

Her lips curved into a wicked grin. "Let's see if you can still say that after tomorrow's workout."

He came closer, his eyes taking in her provocative running outfit. "Ooo," he whispered, reaching out to run his fingers along her jaw, "that sounds ominous."

She fought the immediate response within her body. "Take your h____ __ ____ _____ experience _____

"You know ____ _____ ___ __ ___ __ pain, no gain."

Dear Reader:

Welcome to Silhouette Romance—experience the magic of the wonderful world where two people fall in love. Meet heroines who will make you cheer for their happiness and heroes (be they the boy next door or a handsome, mysterious stranger) who will win your heart. Silhouette Romance novels reflect the magic of love—sweeping you away with stories that will make you laugh and cry; heartwarming, poignant stories that will move you time and time again.

In the next few months, we're publishing romances by many of your all-time favorites such as Diana Palmer, Brittany Young, Annette Broadrick and many others. Your response to these authors and other authors in Silhouette Romance has served as a touchstone for us, and we're pleased to bring you more books with Silhouette's distinctive medley of charm, wit and—above all—*romance*.

During 1991, we have many special events planned. Don't miss our WRITTEN IN THE STARS series. Each month in 1991, we're proud to present readers with a book that focuses on the hero—and his astrological sign.

I hope you'll enjoy this book and all of the stories to come. Come home to romance—Silhouette Romance—for always!

Sincerely,

Tara Gavin
Senior Editor

DONNA CLAYTON

Taking Love in Stride

Published by Silhouette Books New York

America's Publisher of Contemporary Romance

To my parents,
Lewis and Doris Montgomery,
with love and appreciation

SILHOUETTE BOOKS
300 E. 42nd St., New York, N.Y. 10017

TAKING LOVE IN STRIDE

ISBN: 0-373-08781-0

First Silhouette Books printing March 1991

Books by Donna Clayton

Silhouette Romance

Mountain Laurel #720
Taking Love in Stride #781

DONNA CLAYTON

spent her youth visiting a multitude of imaginary places with the help of scores of wonderful books. Her joy of reading turned into a joy of writing. Now, she spends her days creating her own imaginary places and bringing to life characters she hopes her readers will come to love.

Living in Newark, Delaware, with her husband and her two sons, Donna thoroughly enjoys the time they spend hiking, skiing and watching old movies together. She still delights in her love of reading and has gladly passed this entertaining addiction to her children. Donna also collects cookbooks, old and new, and even uses them now and then.

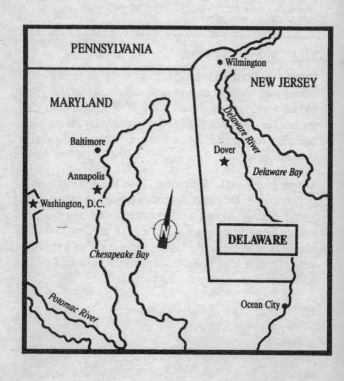

Chapter One

Andrea O'Connor briskly strode the length of the tiled corridor, her ever-present whistle swinging wildly against her chest. What she craved more than anything was to step out of her hot, sticky running clothes and into a cool shower. She'd worked the school's track runners to their limit and, in the process, had gotten a pretty good workout herself. But before she could even think about her own wants and needs, a problem had to be taken care of. Immediately.

Reprimanding students was not something she enjoyed, but if her job as a teacher and coach taught her anything, it was that teenagers needed limits. Andrea knew her kids had to learn that when they overstepped the bounds, there were repercussions to be faced. This particular pupil had thrust her big toe across the boundary line more than once, and Andrea was determined it wouldn't happen again.

Andrea stopped in the art room doorway, momentarily taken aback by the barrage of colors and textures before her. A huge, nearly completed papiermâché Chinese dragon leered at her from the ceiling, its golden eyes and black brows drawn into a fierce frown. A hundred different projects in various stages of development were scattered around the room. The faint traces of turpentine, paint and damp clay that mingled in the air were so different from the familiar smell of the locker room—stale sweat and sneakers—she was so used to.

Denise was perched on a high stool in front of an easel, so engrossed in the colors on the canvas that she didn't even hear her coach enter the room.

Sidestepping a modern sculpture that looked suspiciously like two garbage-can lids wired together, Andrea's shoulder brushed against a shelf. A small round of crimped tin clattered to the floor.

"Miss O'Connor!" Denise plunked her brush into a glass jar of paint thinner so quickly that the jar tipped precariously. "Am I late for practice again? I'm sorry."

"Denise, practice is over."

"Over?" Denise's surprised gaze rose in search of the clock on the wall.

"Over," Andrea repeated. "I think we need to talk."

"But it won't happen again..."

"I know it won't." Andrea's voice dropped. "Because you're off the team."

Andrea watched Denise's throat work in an effort to swallow.

"You can't do that." Denise's eyes held a plea.

"Oh, yes, I can," Andrea said firmly. "And I have."

"But I *have* to be part of the team!"

"That's just it, you're not 'part of the team.' A team works together. Practices together. You've been late for practice more times than I can count, and you've missed two altogether. I've warned you over and over." Andrea took a breath. "Denise, there are rules. And you've broken them. Now it's time to pay the price."

"But you don't understand." Denise's eyes widened in panic. "My dad's going to be furious."

A small frown planted itself in Andrea's brow. "I don't see how this has anything to do with your father. We're discussing a commitment *you* made."

"The only reason I'm on the stupid team...uh, I'm sorry, Miss O'Connor. The only reason I'm on the track team is because my father wants me on the track team."

Andrea's frown deepened. She knew that Denise had no desire to be on the team, but thought the girl was keeping up the stubborn pretense in an attempt to reach the common teenage goals of being popular and visible. Now, from what Denise was saying, the root of the problem was something, or rather, someone completely different.

Andrea knew from personal experience what could happen when parents pushed their kids into doing things they had no desire to do. Frustration, anger and a slow but steady eating away of the child's self-esteem was all it achieved. It had taken Andrea several of her adult years to figure out that she was not put on this earth to make her impossible-to-please father happy.

"Denise, I can't believe your father is insisting that you participate in sports. He's never been to any of the track meets. It's your grandfather who always comes to cheer us on." Andrea remembered the gentleman confined to a wheelchair who never missed a meet.

"Dad travels a lot, so he can't come," Denise explained. "But he thinks my being on the team will teach me all about competition." Denise made a face. "And, he says, healthy competition is what the business world is all about."

"Denise, as long as I've known you, you've never shown an inkling of business aspiration. You're in this art room every minute you can spare." Andrea's head tilted and her eyebrows rose admonishingly as she added, "And quite a few that you can't."

Andrea's eyes swept from the girl to the painting she was working on. The power and vitality of the colors on the canvas surprised her. "You're good," she said. "You're really good. I can almost hear the crashing of the waves and the rumbling thunder. Denise—" Andrea turned back to her student "—doesn't your father know that you can learn 'healthy competition' with your art? There are all kinds of contests. In fact, the school is sponsoring one this month. Have you entered?"

"Oh, no! I couldn't. I couldn't do that . . ." Her voice trailed off and her hands darted with quick jerky motion as she replaced the caps on tubes of paint and wiped her pallet clean.

"Well, why not?"

Andrea knew by Denise's nervous tidying and the girl's refusal to meet her coach's gaze that something was wrong here, something serious. Reaching out, Andrea placed a quelling hand on Denise's forearm.

"Denise," she softly said. "I asked why not?"

Denise's eyes rose reluctantly. "He doesn't know," she whispered.

"Doesn't know?" Andrea watched Denise drape a white sheet over the entire easel. "Your father doesn't know about your painting?"

Her chin lowering, Denise swished her fan brush around in the jar of golden liquid, wiped off her pallet knife and threw it into her paint case before snapping it shut. "Look, Miss O'Connor, I have to go. *Please* give me another chance. I *promise*..."

Andrea shook her head. "Denise, I can't do that."

Denise took a deep breath as she picked up her case and stuffed it in the bottom of a large duffel bag, taking pains to hide it underneath her school books. "Well, I'm in for it," she replied miserably. "And don't be surprised if my dad comes in to see you."

A small spontaneous smile twitched on the corners of Andrea's mouth. Teens treated every event in their lives as extremely grave, monumental.

"It's not as bad as you think. Go home and talk to your dad."

"I can't!" Denise almost shouted her conviction. "You don't understand. I can't tell my dad."

Denise picked up her duffel bag and rushed from the room. Andrea stared at the empty doorway for a long time, frowning. Was Denise overreacting to how she thought her father would respond to her being dropped from the team? Or could her father, indeed, be forcing her to run track in some vain effort for his daughter to learn "healthy competition"?

Andrea couldn't tolerate pushy, overbearing parents whose goals were to raise bright, profit-making, overachieving children. All these parents succeeded in doing was turning their happy, well-adjusted kids into insecure neurotics. She'd love the chance to tell Denise's father exactly what he was doing to his daughter. Diplomatically, of course. Her frown was replaced with a slow, devilish smile. She hoped Mr. Powers *would* come in to see her. "I'll be waiting for him," she whispered.

When Andrea entered the teacher's lounge the next afternoon, the odor of burned coffee assailed her. Wrinkling her nose, she snapped off the coffee machine. She picked up the glass pot, grimaced at the thick black crust in its bottom and set the pot in the sink. She placed a tea bag in a cup and poured hot water over it.

It had been a long day. One of her students, a junior who should have known better, sprained her wrist while clowning around in gym class. And Andrea had found herself hard pressed to be patient with a group of giggling freshmen as she tried to explain the workings of the female anatomy during health class. Add to that an after-school track practice that had been grueling—she'd had to work the team extra hard due to the upcoming track meet—and it was all more than enough to equal a rough day.

She'd been thinking about Denise Powers off and on all day long. Andrea had expected a call from the school's secretary that Mr. Powers had made an appointment to meet with her. She'd spent every spare moment planning exactly what she wanted to say to him. That poor girl, she thought, having to live with that pushy brute.

But, she hadn't gotten a call or a message. He hadn't made an appointment, so Denise must have been mistaken about her father's reaction to the news of her being cut from the team. Either that, or the man didn't care a wit, the unfeeling worm.

Andrea looked at her watch. She had a five-thirty appointment with Mr. Scott, the school's principal, in twenty minutes. She was feeling the need to relax for every one of those minutes before she urged with him one more time about the purchase of new track equipment. She'd enjoy this cup of tea at her desk, then tackle Mr. Scott.

On her way back to her office, she came up behind a tall, dark-haired man who was standing at the crossway of the halls. When he turned his head to stare up one corridor, Andrea's breath caught in her throat at the sight of the most gorgeous profile she'd ever laid eyes on.

His features were sharp, as though they were chiseled in stone. His ebony hair was smoothed straight back from his forehead. Andrea focused on this strong chin and a roguish, quarter-inch scar that was flaunted there. Probably a football injury, she thought. Those were definitely football shoulders straining against that white dress shirt. Her gaze returned to his face, bronzed skin covering high cheekbones, a square jawline and sensuously full lips. And his eyes! His eyes were chips of polished onyx.

Realizing he had turned toward her, Andrea's face flushed; she was sure he was aware of her intense scrutiny. Everything else was forgotten as she was pulled into the black depths of his piercing stare. There was nothing subtle about the awareness that was ricocheting between them.

It took every ounce of control she could muster, but she succeeded in lowering her eyes to glance into the cup that she held in her hand. She couldn't help but notice her breathlessness, as though she'd just finished a long run. God, what was the matter with her?

She jerked her head up to look at him, hoping he was oblivious to the state she was in. No such luck. His slow, lazy smile told her he was not only aware, he was enjoying it!

Sucking in a deep breath, she squared her shoulders. She hadn't the slightest idea who he was, but she looked a fool for no one.

"You seem lost," she commented, happy with the strength and clarity of her voice. "Can I help you?"

"I'm looking for the principal's office."

Although his request was spoken with candor, those black eyes held more than a hint of an I-know-you-want-me look that infuriated Andrea. She cleared her throat, trying to ease the tightness her anger and agitation was causing and pointed up the hall.

"Make the first left, there. Mr. Scott's office is the second door on the left."

The man lowered his chin in a tiny bow of gratitude, and Andrea's eyes darted once more to that devastatingly sexy scar. When he lifted his head, she nodded toward him and turned to walk in the opposite direction.

A sixth sense told her he was watching. Her anger flared anew, knowing that *he* was now scrutinizing *her*. She straightened her back, suddenly conscious of the natural sway of her hips.

When she reached her office door, she gave in to the irresistible temptation to turn around. She sighed at the sight of the empty hallway and was filled with a fleeting sense of self-reproof, knowing the sigh was more from disappointment rather than relief.

She sat down at her desk and sipped at her tepid, tasteless tea. Now she had only fifteen minutes to plan her strategy to get the new equipment for the physical-education department. The small private school was in dire need of new track equipment and had been for some time, but the school's principal didn't see it that way. She knew she needed to approach Mr. Scott from a new angle, her straightforward presentation of the facts having failed so miserably in the past.

Closing her eyes to think, her mind was overpowered by a black, hypnotic gaze. Damn! The man's face was crystal clear in her head. Who was he? she wondered. Could he possibly be the new math teacher? She remembered the potent power and commanding strength that exuded from him, and she knew he'd never be content stuck behind a desk teaching equations all day.

She shook her head, trying to clear the dark stranger from her thoughts. She needed to plan for her meeting with Mr. Scott.

"Miss O'Connor," Sylvia Green, the school's secretary, called over the intercom in a harried whisper. "Would you come to the office . . . right away?"

That's odd, Andrea thought, the woman sounded upset. Nothing flustered the indomitable Sylvia. Even when her boss was on the warpath, Sylvia remained calm and composed.

Glancing at her watch, Andrea frowned. Something *must* be up. There were still nine minutes before her scheduled appointment. And if there was anything Mr. Scott stressed, it was punctuality—not two minutes early or two minutes late.

Andrea ran a hand over her cap of silky blond hair as she hurried to the office. The heels of her white shoes tapped hollowly in the empty corridor. She smoothed the bodice of her pink dress, the full skirt falling softly over her slim hips. Mr. Scott constantly complained that just because she was a gym teacher, she needn't look like one, so, whenever she had to meet with him, she took pains with her appearance.

She wondered what was stewing in the office. Rats! she thought. Mr. Scott's probably going to give me a tongue-lashing because Sally was hurt in class today. Andrea knew that if he became too preoccupied with raking her over the coals, they would never get the chance to discuss the new track equipment. She wouldn't have put it past him to have planned it that way. Well, she was determined that he *would* discuss the track equipment with her this afternoon, whether he wanted to or not!

"Hi, Sylvia." Andrea smiled brightly as she entered the office. Noting the woman's stark coloring, she felt intense stirrings of unease flutter in her stomach.

"He in there?" Andrea asked, pointing at Mr. Scott's closed door.

Sylvia nodded.

"Is everything all right?"

Sylvia slowly shook her head.

As Andrea turned the handle on the door, she heard Mr. Scott's usually forceful voice take on an extremely accommodating quality that was almost a whine, something she'd never heard before.

"You can be assured that everything will be put right," Andrea heard the principal say.

"You're damned right it will!" a deep threatening voice boomed.

Andrea took a breath to calm her jittery insides. What could this possibly have to do with her? Knocking twice, she pushed into Mr. Scott's office.

"Miss O'Connor." Mr. Scott stood, greeting her with an icy glare. "Come in."

She took one step into the room. She'd never seen him in such a state. Mr. Scott's usual brash cockiness had disintegrated completely. A curving line of sweat had gathered over his top lip.

The atmosphere in the room was thick with strain. Andrea's eyes flew to the other occupant of the office, wanting to know what kind of person could turn her pompous boss into a whipped puppy.

"*You're* Coach O'Connor?"

Andrea never knew whether it was the man's sarcastic tone or the sight of the "dark stranger" himself that made her stop dead in her tracks. She was momentarily stunned into silence. Who was this man? And what could he want with her? She swallowed the questions and took another step toward the two men.

"I'm Andrea O'Connor, yes." She extended her hand. "And you're...?"

"Ian Powers," he said.

His big hand enveloped her small one. Heat shot through her fingers and palm, past her wrist and right up her arm. Shocked by the sensation, Andrea jerked her hand from his grasp and absently rubbed it against her thigh.

Powers, Powers. She knew that name. Why couldn't she think straight?

"Denise's father," Mr. Scott emphasized.

Denise's father! Her foggy brain cleared instantly. How dare this man go over her head to the school's principal before speaking to her first!

"Denise's father," Ian Powers repeated. His eyes gleamed with a hint of laughter. He was laughing at her! Andrea's throat tightened with familiar anger, the same anger she'd felt when he'd given her that identical laughing look in the hall.

"You dropped Denise from the track team," Mr. Scott accused. "Mr. Powers wants Denise put back on the team. I told him you'd comply."

Andrea stared at Mr. Scott. A sheen of perspiration had erupted on his high forehead, making it shiny and slick. Andrea's eyes narrowed as she realized that Mr. Scott was trying to bully her into doing as he said.

This isn't right, she thought, her nails digging into the soft flesh of her palm. A principal was supposed to assume his teachers were in the right and back them up, not turn on them just because a parent applied a little heat. Mr. Scott hadn't even bothered to find out why she'd dropped Denise from the team in the first place.

"I'm sorry, but that's not possible." She was pleased at how self-assured her words sounded, because she definitely didn't feel that way.

"Miss O'Connor!" Mr. Scott's voice cracked with surprise.

She looked from Mr. Scott's wide, shocked eyes to Ian Powers's granite-hard ones. Taking a deep breath, she spoke with as much authority as she could summon. "I'd like to remind both of you that *I* am the coach of the track team, and *I* am the one who decides who will be on the team and who will not. If either of you had bothered to ask, you would know that I had a perfectly valid reason for doing what I did."

The tension between the three of them was so heavy, Andrea could almost feel it pressing against her. Neither man spoke. Glancing back at Mr. Scott, she watched his Adam's apple bob frantically. He's pitiful, she thought. He struts around this school like he's king, but let a parent come in and complain and he turns into a lump of warm clay. It was no wonder the teachers called him Fainthearted Franny. Even though Andrea had never experienced this side of him before, she now knew that Francis Scott was a fraud.

She focused on Ian Powers. It was not so easy to meet his hard, threatening stare. Who was he that he thought he could come in here and push everyone around?

When she first knew she might have to meet with Denise's father, she had decided that, as a teacher, it would be best to use tact and diplomacy when she explained the situation. But after the way he'd barged in, demanding his own way of things, she no longer felt she was under that obligation. This man needed to be set straight, and she was glad to be the one to do it.

"Mr. Powers, if you'd like to follow me to my office, I'd be happy to explain exactly why I refuse to let Denise run."

"Miss O'Connor—" Ian Powers's voice was cold, his steely eyes fierce "—you are in no position to refuse my daughter anything. As I've already pointed out to Mr. Scott, I pay this school a staggering amount of money each month, and I will not stand by and see Denise denied the opportunity of participating in any activity this school has to offer. Especially one she thrives on!"

It was as though a rage-filled balloon exploded inside her. Andrea's fingernails dug into her palms and her eyes narrowed ominously. This idiot macho creep didn't even know his own daughter, for God's sake!

"I'm going to let you in on a little secret, Mr. Powers." Andrea knew her face was red with fury, she could feel the heat. "It's pushy, obnoxious parents like you that—"

"Miss O'Connor!" Mr. Scott checked her before she could continue.

"It's quite all right," Ian Powers remarked. "I'd like to hear everything Miss O'Connor has to say. It's much more satisfying when I get what I want *after* the opposition has thoroughly embarrassed themselves stating their opinion of why I can't have it."

She looked at his smugly confident expression and seethed inside. He's intolerable! Andrea thought. A first-class jerk!

"There's no need for you to suffer through any opinions Miss O'Connor might have." Mr. Scott straightened his tie, trying to regain some of his battered dignity. "I've already assured you that every-

thing will be set right, with or without Miss
O'Connor's approval.''

Ian Powers gave the principal a thin, icy smile. "I
don't think you understand. I insist she have her say."

They were talking about Andrea as though she were
invisible. Or worst yet, some mindless bubblehead!
She wouldn't have it!

But, before she could even open her mouth to
speak, Ian Powers had grasped her by the elbow and
propelled her toward the door.

"Be assured, Mr. Scott, I'll get back to you." Ian
Powers opened the door and practically dragged Andrea from the room.

As she was being pulled through the secretary's office and into the hall, she saw Sylvia ooze down into
her chair, so as not to be noticed. Andrea had seen
students take the same action a thousand times as they
tried to avoid being called on for an answer. This
whole situation was ridiculous!

"Which way?" he asked.

"I must say, it's pretty sad." Andrea yanked her elbow from his grasp and smoothed the wrinkled material of her sleeve. "Your daughter has attended this
school for three and a half years and you can't even
find the gymnasium, the biggest room in the building."

"It's not important that I be able to find it. Denise
is the student. It's important that she be able to find
it."

His cavalier attitude toward the point she was trying
to make fanned the flame of Andrea's anger. She
started down the corridor at a brisk pace, hoping to

leave him behind, but he quickly caught and matched her stride.

"The first thing I'd like to say right up front—" Andrea kept her eyes straight ahead "—is that there was no reason for you to go over my head on this. We could have avoided all this unpleasantness if you had only come to see me instead of Mr. Scott. He doesn't even know the situation! I would have been more than happy to explain every—"

"Whoa, whoa." Mr. Powers stopped short, forcing Andrea to turn and face him. "It was never my intention to go over your head. And I'm sorry if you got that impression. I just returned from business, and I have to leave again tomorrow."

Andrea couldn't help but shake her head. Just like Robert, she thought. Her father had traveled, too, breezing into town just long enough to dictate how she would live her young life, but never long enough to establish a loving father-daughter relationship. She had never felt close enough to him to call him Dad, or even Father. It had always been Robert. And Ian Powers seemed to be treating his daughter in the same enforcing-yet-detached fashion.

"Robert? Who's Robert?" His surprised question snapped her back to the present.

Had she really spoken her father's name aloud?

"No one important, Mr. Powers. Just a busy man I know who's a lot like you. A traveling businessman, so to speak." She heard the condemnation in her voice and she raised her downcast eyes to see his reaction. A tiny twinge of guilt sparked inside her when he cocked his head in an offended manner.

"It's because of my business and all the traveling I do that Denise has the opportunity to attend this school at all."

"I didn't mean to be rude, Mr. Powers. How you live your life and conduct your family affairs is none of my business. Not, that is, until it interferes with my job. I can't help but ask one burning question. Why are you pushing Denise so hard to do something that she has no desire to do? It's not healthy. It's not—"

"Pushing?" he interrupted, incredulous. "That's the second time you've used that word. You want to explain what the hell you mean? My kid loves—"

"Open your eyes, Mr. Powers! Your 'kid' is a sixteen-year-old young woman. A young woman who's only just beginning to discover the person she wants to be."

She watched a deep frown crease his brow.

"Are you telling me that I don't know my own daughter?"

"I'm telling you that you can't live life through Denise. If you have a desire to run, then arrange your busy schedule so you can do it, and let Denise live her own life, follow her own dreams."

"What kind of father do you think I am?" His face contorted with disgust. "Never mind, I can see by the look in your eyes." He straightened suddenly, his shoulders squaring. "I have never in my life pushed Denise into doing anything!" His eyes gleamed with bitterness. "What makes you such an authority on parenting, anyway? I can see by that bare ring finger on your left hand, *Miss* O'Connor, that you've been married a decade and have a brood of kids of your own at home."

Andrea's whole body tensed under his attack. "Mr. Powers, I spend more time with these kids than most parents. And I'd be more than willing to bet my best pair of running shoes that you haven't spent half as much time with your daughter as I have!"

"I spend plenty of quality time—"

Andrea cut him off with a harsh, humorless laugh. "'Quality time.' That is the catch phrase of the day, isn't it? If you ask me, it's the cop-out excuse of the day, too."

"You can't know what it's like to be a parent until you *are* one!"

"Mr. Powers." Andrea kept her voice as calm as possible. It was time this man was told the truth. "I can *prove* to you that I know Denise better than you do." She stood there staring at him a moment before changing direction abruptly to stalk off toward the art room.

Chapter Two

Where was she going, now? Ian watched in bewilderment as his daughter's track coach stomped past him.

Damn it, he thought. He was going to get Denise back on that track team if it was the last thing he did. And after colliding head-on with this vivacious fireball, he thought it very well may be!

As he followed her, his eye caught the rhythm of her hemline swishing against her flexing calf muscles. In spite of his angry determination to see that his daughter was given her due, he couldn't help but appreciate the sway of the trim body in front of him. He'd never come up against anyone quite like Andrea O'Connor. In fact, he couldn't remember the last time someone had stood up to him the way she had.

He had learned that in the business world it was necessary to be assured and forceful to succeed. And those same traits, he had found, came in handy in circumstances such as this, when he had less time to deal with a problem than he might like.

His most tyrannical glare, the same one that had intimidated the school's principal, hadn't begun to faze Miss O'Connor. Her chin had raised determinedly, and she'd even had the audacity to insult him right there in front of her boss! And her eyes—the way they'd turned to icy-blue shards of cold determination.

But he'd been stunned by the sparks that arched between them in spite of their angry confrontation, the same shock of electricity he'd felt when they'd encountered each other for the first time in the hallway. He had never been so attracted to a complete stranger.

He took a deep breath, determined to push the intrusive thoughts out of his mind. This woman was standing between him and his daughter's happiness, and he wouldn't have it.

How could she possibly claim to know Denise better than he? Granted, he was away on business quite often. But Denise was his daughter! And while he was away, his father was always there for her. Miss O'Connor, Ian decided, was talking out her ear.

I can prove it. Her words reverberated in his head. And here he was following her like a lamb to slaughter. What was she up to? He wouldn't be railroaded! He knew what Denise's rights were and he intended to stand up for them.

His thoughts drifted to this afternoon, when this whole mess had started. He'd just gotten in from Chicago when his distraught father had met him at the front door.

"That crazy teacher kicked Denise off the track team," his father had shouted. "You know she wants to run track more than anything. Now, you go in there and see that things are set right."

Denise was at the mall with friends, so Ian hadn't had a chance to talk with her. And since he had to leave for Boston in the morning, he felt he had to go to the school immediately.

Soon after meeting Mr. Scott, Ian knew the problem wasn't as big as he had first thought. In fact, the school's principal agreed to his demands at once.

But upon meeting the feisty track coach, Ian found the problem swelling out of proportion again. He could see right away that Andrea O'Connor was not going to be nearly as yielding as Mr. Scott.

Still several steps behind her, Ian recognized her set state of mind from her brisk pace and her clenched fists.

He played follow the leader around two more corners before Miss O'Connor disappeared through what he thought was a classroom doorway. When he followed her through, he was confused. This isn't a classroom, he thought, this is some sort of storeroom. Why would she bring him here? He was amazed at the vast array of junk strewn about.

As he scratched his head and looked around, he inadvertently kicked two garbage can lids, sending them clattering across the floor.

"Be careful!" Miss O'Connor snapped. "Some student has worked hard on that art project."

Ian gaped at the mess he'd made of the supposed structure. "Art project?" he asked, trying to set the lids back into position. "This is the art room?"

His eyes were drawn to the ceiling, where a tired old Mardi Gras dragon was hung, its tissue paper wrinkled and torn. Blobs of clay were lining the gray metal shelves. Ian squinted at a vase that was covered with small squares of masking tape. This was art?

"Over here." She directed him toward an easel covered with a white drop cloth. He stared at the painting she uncovered for several long seconds. From what he'd seen, it was the only piece in the room that could be classified as art. He was surprised at the apparent talent of the painter. The dark stormy sea depicted on the canvas was turbulent, powerful.

"It's beautiful," he finally said.

"It's Denise's."

He looked at Miss O'Connor. "You're kidding, right?"

"No. I'm not."

His eyes traveled back to the canvas. "I can't believe it." He took a step closer. "Are you sure?"

"Positive."

He couldn't pull his gaze away from the painting resting on the easel.

"It's really good."

"It's better than good," she remarked.

"You're right," he said as the two of them stood staring at the painting. "I had no idea." He shook his head. "I know I shouldn't be so surprised. Denise's mother was a talented painter." He shrugged his shoulders, not taking his eyes off the canvas. "It's just that Denise never hinted..." His voice trailed off.

"Denise spends every available minute right here. She doesn't want to run. Why do you think I dropped her from the team?" Andrea asked, eyebrows raised in question. "Because she never came to practice. When I confronted her, she told me that the only reason she went out for the team at all is because you wanted her to learn healthy competition."

" 'Healthy competition'?" His brow creased with confusion. "Where in the world did she hear that?"

"I don't know where she heard it, Mr. Powers. But she believes it. And if you're not the one forcing her into running, then someone else is."

A glaring light clicked on in Ian's head. His father used to run. But that was years ago, before Denise was even born, before the accident that had paralyzed him. His father couldn't be behind this... Or could he? Ian was damned sure going to find out!

He looked back at the painting and shook his head. How could he have been so blind to his own daughter's talent?

"Listen. Thank you . . . for showing me this." He gestured toward the easel.

"It was nothing, Mr. Powers."

Her tone was smug, but it didn't offend him. She had every right. She'd said she knew Denise better than he, and she'd proven it without a shadow of a doubt.

"I guess I owe you an apology."

"No apology necessary. Just making you see things my way makes me very happy." Placing her index finger on her chin, she asked, "What was that you said earlier? 'It's much more satisfying to get what you want after the opposition has thoroughly embarrassed themselves . . .' "

"Okay, okay." Ian laughed. "There's no need to rub it in."

He watched her lips tilt up in a smile.

"I couldn't resist."

As she turned to replace the cover over the easel, Ian's eyes were drawn once more to his daughter's painting. He sighed and slowly shook his head. What was Denise thinking to keep this from him? And why did she feel compelled to run on the track team? Other questions began to gather in his head, questions he was bent on finding answers to.

"Thanks again," he said. "I'm going home to find out exactly what's going on." Turning toward the door, he stalked from the room.

Andrea was awakened by a warm, wet tongue lapping at her jaw. When she opened her eyes, the German shepherd sat back on its haunches and whined.

"Good morning, Gunther. You need to go out?" Sitting on the edge of her bed, Andrea stroked the dog's silken coat. She glanced over at the clock and saw that in two minutes the alarm was set to go off. Ruffling Gunther's ears, she said, "I swear, you must be able to tell time. Come on, then."

She opened the sliding glass doors in the kitchen and watched as Gunther bounded out into the yard. The cool spring breeze brushed against her face and she breathed deeply. The trees were beginning to bud, and the crocuses filled the otherwise brown garden with bursts of yellow, red and white. The grass was beginning to turn green, and everything smelled fresh and new.

Springtime always made her feel light and happy. She even felt pleased with the outcome of her confrontation with Ian Powers yesterday afternoon. She may not have liked the man much, but she did have to give him credit for admitting his mistake. He also seemed determined to talk with Denise about their problem.

"And that's just what they need to do—talk," Andrea whispered.

She went back into her bedroom and started getting ready for work, making a mental note to see Denise today and ask how things had gone.

As it turned out, Andrea didn't have to seek out Denise at all. When she walked down the hall toward her office, she saw the teenager standing by the locker-room door. The tragic look on Denise's face made her frown.

"What's wrong?" she asked.

"I've been waiting for you. I need to talk. I need to get back on the team. Dad says I should spend my time painting, but I feel bad for Pops—"

"Wait a minute, slow down," Andrea said, waving her free hand. "Come in here so we can discuss this calmly." Fumbling with her keys, she unlocked her office door and pushed it open. She dropped her canvas case on her desk and slipped out of her jacket. "Now, sit down, take a deep breath and start at the beginning."

"Dad found out about my painting," Denise began. "I don't know how, but—"

"That was my fault," Andrea admitted.

"No, it's all right. He wasn't angry like I thought he would be."

"I don't understand why you thought he'd be angry in the first place."

Denise lowered her eyes. "My mom painted. She was really talented. But she died when I was a little girl and I was afraid that my painting might make Dad think of her and make him sad."

She lifted her face to look at Andrea. "But everything's okay. He wants me to paint. In fact, he took me out last night and bought me lots of supplies. When we came home, Dad and my granddad started arguing." Denise slid to the edge of her chair. "You see, Pops was the one wanting me on the track team. He kept blaming it on Dad. When Dad found out, he hit the roof. Dad told Pops to stop forcing me to run."

Andrea cupped her chin in her palm. "Why would your grandfather do such a thing, Denise?" she asked.

"Miss O'Connor, before Pops had his accident, he was a runner, a good runner, one of the best in Delaware. He helped organize the very first half marathon ever run in Wilmington." Denise took a deep breath. "He won that first race."

She rested her clasped hands on Andrea's desk and leaned even closer. "This year is the twentieth anniversary of the Wilmington Challenge. And Pops has been asked to present the winners their trophies. Pops wanted me to participate in the Challenge."

Andrea watched Denise's features fill with sympathy for her grandfather.

"I want to run for him," the girl said.

"Denise..." Andrea's voice was soft with understanding. "We've already talked about the importance of living your own life. You have to realize that you can't run this race in place of your grandfather. He'll still be confined to his wheelchair, he'll still be unable to run."

"Please, Miss O'Connor," Denise pleaded fervently. "I know Pops won't be able feel the pavement under his feet or the wind in his face. But he'll know I'm out there. And he'll know I'm doing it for him." Denise's eyes gleamed with tears. "It's important to him, Miss O'Connor. I want to do this for Pops."

Andrea was so moved by the girl's passion that her own eyes misted with emotion. She was silent while she mulled over Denise's plight. But it didn't take her long to decide what to do.

"So, you want me to put you back on the team so you can train?"

"Oh, please. You'll see, things will be different. I'll never miss a practice. I'll never be late." Denise was sitting on the edge of her seat.

A grin twisted Andrea's lips. "Well, I *have* been short a long-distance runner since you've been gone...."

"Oh, thank you!" Denise's face lit up with her gratitude.

"Wait a minute. What about your painting? And what about your father?"

It was as though a dark cloud descended on both of them. And it took several seconds for Denise to respond.

"The painting's no problem. I can always find time for that." She hesitated. "But I don't plan to tell Dad—I don't want him to know."

"Denise," Andrea admonished, "you can't lie to your father."

"I won't be lying," Denise said. "Just not telling. Anyway, he'll blame Pops! You can't imagine how angry he was last night."

Oh, yes, I can, Andrea thought. "Look, I can't make you tell your dad what you're planning to do, but I think you should. Tell him exactly what you told me. He'll understand." But will he? she silently wondered. "Denise, don't ask me to lie for you, because I won't."

"That won't be a problem," Denise declared stubbornly. She gathered her books and headed toward the door. "You won't need to lie or anything, 'cause you won't see him."

"Practice is at three-thirty sharp!" Andrea called to the empty doorway.

You won't see him. Denise's words echoed in Andrea's head. Maybe Denise was right and she wouldn't encounter Ian again. In the three-plus years she'd been Denise's teacher, she'd met the girl's father only once, but it was a meeting she'd never forget. Her body trembled as she remembered the electricity that had crackled between them. As much as she hoped Denise's prediction would come true, somehow she was sure that she wouldn't be that lucky.

Ian's mind wasn't on the heavy afternoon traffic of Interstate 95. As he headed out of the city toward his daughter's school, last night's tumultuous scene with his father thrust itself once again to the forefront of his thoughts. He was puzzled by his family's behavior. So much so that he'd canceled today's business trip, knowing he needed time to figure this whole thing out.

Denise, a painter! The very idea was astonishing, but he knew he shouldn't be surprised. Denise's mother had been extremely talented, hadn't she? He shook his head. Maybe it had been memories of Sondra that had kept Denise from telling anyone about her painting.

But Denise had talent. There was no denying it. He knew it the moment he'd seen her work yesterday. He should definitely speak to Denise's art teacher.

But it was his father's actions that bothered him most. Ian knew his father had had a hard time adjusting to being paralyzed. Who wouldn't? The whole family had had to adjust. But Ian had thought Harry had adapted well to the change in life-style.

Now, he was shocked to find out that his father was still emotionally unsettled by his paralysis. Harry had been coercing Denise into running track and planting ideas into her head that Ian was the one demanding it. It was all so unlike the kind, honest man he knew his father to be.

Harry's actions only proved to Ian how very important this upcoming race was to his dad. And after spending the entire day weighing the facts—Denise's disinterest in running and Harry's desire to have a family member run in the Wilmington Challenge—Ian had decided exactly what to do. He'd run in the race himself.

And since he hadn't the slightest idea what training for a long-distance run involved, it was only logical for him to ask Andrea O'Connor for help. It was an excellent excuse to meet the high-spirited woman again and see if there really had been anything to the instant awareness he'd felt when he was with her yesterday.

Andrea entered her office from her private washroom and planted her sneakered foot on the green vinyl seat of her desk chair. Pulling the laces tight, she tied them in a double knot. She picked up the silver whistle off her desk and slipped the braided cord over her head.

She was looking forward to a good, tough practice. The team had a meet in two weeks and, if she could whip these kids into shape, they had a very good shot at winning.

Scooping up her stopwatch and clipboard, she studied the names listed. Her eyes stopped when they reached "Powers, Denise." Andrea smiled. Denise had been on time for practice, a few minutes early, in fact. Remembering the girl's plea for help in training, Andrea was proud that Denise had stuck with her end of the bargain.

She needed to speak to Denise again, though, about telling her father that she was back on the team. Even if Andrea never saw Ian again, she wasn't comfortable with his not knowing that his daughter was running on the track team. Besides, it was against school policy for a student to participate in any sport without parental consent. Yes, she'd have to talk to Denise right away.

A sharp rap sounded on the door of her office that led directly into the locker room.

"Miss O'Connor?" Denise barged into the room.

"Denise," Andrea said, "just the person I wanted to see."

"Miss O'Connor!" Denise was frantically shaking her head, looking across the room at the door that led out into the hall.

"What?" Andrea asked. But as she took in the girl's flushed, anxious face, her smiled faded. "What is it?"

Denise gulped in air and tried to swallow. "I ran up from the track as soon as I saw him. My dad. He's coming."

"Your dad...?" Andrea's voice trailed off as a thousand butterflies started flailing wildly in her stomach. Her own eyes darted toward the door. "Well, maybe he's coming to see you."

Denise shook her head. "He doesn't even know I'm here."

"Well, Mr. Scott, then," Andrea said.

Denise jerked her head back and forth again. "No, he's headed toward the gym entrance. And he was walking that walk."

"That walk?" Andrea's eyebrows rose and the butterflies in her stomach were joined by a thousand more, all of them flapping furiously.

"Yeah, I've seen it before. He only walks like that when he's on his way to pulverize somebody. It's his determined walk. Somebody's in for it." Denise hesitated, inching toward the door. "And, Miss O'Connor, I think it's you."

"Wait a minute. Wait a minute." With her free hand, Andrea grabbed Denise by the sleeve of her track suit. "You need to tell your dad that you're back on the team. And now's as good a time as any."

"No, no!" Denise was back to urgently shaking her head. "You don't know how angry he was last night. He wasn't just upset, he was *furious!*" She said the last word in an emphasized whisper, her eyes round as saucers as she pulled her sleeve from between her coach's fingers and slipped out the locker-room door.

As Denise pulled the door closed behind her, Andrea fumbled with her stopwatch and clipboard, grabbed hold of the knob on her side of the door and tried to wrestle it open. The clipboard clattered to the floor, her pencil skittering across the shiny tiling, but she didn't relinquish her hold on the door handle.

"No, you don't," Andrea said. "You come back in here."

"I'll tell him later, I promise. He needs to cool down first." Denise pulled on the door handle, dragging her teacher along with it.

Suddenly, Andrea realized how ridiculous they must look playing tug-of-war with her office door. She let go of the knob as though it were a hot coal. The door slammed shut and she heard Denise's "oof" of surprise.

What are you doing? she wondered. Why are you so desperate to have Denise with you when her father arrives? What are you afraid of? Ian Powers? She'd handled him quite well yesterday. Then, what was it? She took a deep breath, not wanting to admit the truth. She knew what she was afraid of. It was those vibrations she'd felt the first time she'd ever laid eyes on him. An electricity so strong it had shocked her. She'd never felt anything like it before, and she didn't know how to deal with it; didn't want to deal with it.

"Denise," Andrea called through the closed door, "I will not lie for you." The threat was a last-ditch effort to get Denise to come back into the office so they could face Ian together.

"Okay," Denise said, "then you tell him!"

Andrea rolled her eyes to the ceiling as she listened to Denise scamper out of the locker-room's rear exit. But it was the soft knock on her outer office door that caused the butterflies in her stomach to flutter with renewed vengeance.

Chapter Three

Andrea inhaled deeply. She straightened her nylon
tank top and reached down to snatch her clipboard
and pencil off the floor. Smoothing a hand through
her hair, she tried to calm her racing heart.

*Get a hold of yourself. You can handle this. All you
have to do is calmly listen to what he has to say and
then send him on his way.*

But the sight of his shadow against the frosted glass
and the sound of his knuckles on the wooden door
frame made her throat constrict and her mouth go dry.

"Come in," she croaked.

When he pushed his way into her office, she felt
impelled to take a step back. He stood towering in the
middle of the room, and Andrea realized for the first
time how small her office really was.

His dark gaze struck her almost physically, and
those overpowering vibes that she was dreading

emanated from his confident posture. But she was momentarily thrown by his friendly smile.

"Hello again," he said. "I'm sorry for dropping in on you like this, but I had something I wanted to ask you."

She stared at him a long second. Curiosity about why he was there battled with her desire to escape the strong vibrations she felt radiating from him.

Suddenly conscious of ogling the man, Andrea dropped her embarrassed gaze to her desk. When her eyes stumbled on the stopwatch lying there, her mind cleared.

"Oh, well...see..." she said, glancing at her wristwatch, "I have to be at track practice in five minutes."

"That's great." He sat down on the chair in front of her desk. "I only need three."

"But—"

"Sit, sit," he commanded. "I have a favor to ask."

"But, I really don't have—"

"Would you sit down and listen? You've only given me three minutes."

Andrea's mouth snapped shut, and she lowered herself onto her chair. She couldn't remember giving him anything, let alone three minutes. But witnessing his compelling demeanor, she knew she wouldn't be able to escape him until she heard him out. She stared into his black eyes, silent, waiting.

"I'm going to run the Wilmington Challenge. And you're going to help me."

"What?" If he'd meant to knock her off balance, he'd certainly attained his goal. She'd thought he was going to thank her for telling him of his daughter's artistic talent. Or maybe some plan he'd made to make it easier for Denise to perfect that talent. But his two statements about the Wilmington Challenge had absolutely nothing to do with Denise at all. It took Andrea's breath away.

His announcement to run a half marathon shocked her into an even deeper silence. But his request, no, his *demand* for her assistance struck a spark of anger in her. Here he was, once again, barging in, telling people what they would or wouldn't be doing. Damn the man!

"It's my father," he continued. "He wanted Denise to participate in the run . . ."

Andrea felt a quick stab of guilt at the reminder of Denise being on the track team without her father's knowledge.

". . . And since I've put a stop to that—you and I both know Denise isn't interested in running—I intend to participate in the marathon myself."

So, she thought, he wants to run in the race for his father. The fleeting sense of admiration she felt toward Ian and his noble gesture quickly vanished as she remembered the type of man he was. She might not know him well, but she knew his kind.

He was a dominating businessman, completely immersed in his work, just like her father had been. His wheeling and dealing overrode everything else in his life, even his family's welfare. Somewhere in her reproachful musings, memories of her own father's morbid drive to succeed became mixed with her thoughts of Ian until, finally, she couldn't discern one from the other. All she knew was that this man didn't have it in him to commit himself to anything other than his business.

"Andrea. Andrea, have you been listening to me?"

Ian's voice pulled her back to the present. She took a deep breath and focused on his face.

"Yes, I've been listening."

"Well, what do you say? Will you help me?"

"No," she said bluntly. "I can't." She saw his eyes fill with disappointment.

"But, why?" He paused. Then his face lit with a new idea. "I'll pay you," he offered.

Andrea barely contained a snort of contempt. "I'm not interested in your money. I can't help you."

"You can't?" His friendly manner disappeared as his eyes narrowed scathingly. "Or you won't?"

"It doesn't matter which."

Why was this woman constantly bent on thwarting him? Ian wondered. Yesterday she refused to put Denise back on the track team, and here she was today rejecting a chance to help him do something good, something that would make his father very happy. Granted, she'd been right to take his daughter off the team. But why was she turning him down?

"You're still angry, aren't you?" he asked.

"What are you talking about?"

"You won't help me train—" his voice became louder as his temper heated "—because I went to see Mr. Scott yesterday rather than coming directly to you. I explained my reasons for doing that. Why can't you try to understand?"

Andrea stood. "You're the one who doesn't understand. I am not angry about yesterday. That's not why I won't help you."

"There! You admitted it yourself." He shot up from the chair. "It's not that you can't, it's that you won't. I want to know why."

They glared across the desk at each other, neither willing to back down an inch.

Reprehension built inside Andrea, hot and strong, as she thought about everything she disapproved of in this man. The fear he evoked in his daughter. His absences while on business that left Denise virtually parentless. His ignorance about Denise's talents and desires. The way he barged into the school yesterday. Even his inability to find his way around the school building. And now his arrogant demand that she drop everything to prepare him for a run that he would never have the willpower or the discipline to even train for, let alone finish. All of these tidbits added together could only equal one thing—that Ian's character mirrored her own father's. And that realization filled her with criticism.

"You want the truth?" she challenged.

His expectant silence urged her to continue.

"You don't have what it takes."

She anticipated his affronted anger and was confused by the droll smile he gave her.

"And how have you come to that conclusion?" he asked.

"Let's just say you remind me of someone I knew."

His smile broadened. "That's a dangerous practice, comparing one person to another."

"Nevertheless," she said, "I think it's perfectly natural to use past experiences when planning present actions. And your resemblance to this person from my past leads me to believe that helping you to train would be a waste of my time and effort. Yours, too."

His short bark of laughter wasn't because he was amused, and Andrea could see the tension building in him.

"You're so damned self-righteous," he said. "This person I remind you of wouldn't happen to be this Robert that you mentioned yesterday, would it? The traveling businessman that you spoke of with such disdain? Who was he anyway? An ex-boyfriend? A lover?"

"It doesn't matter!"

"Oh, yes, it does! It does when you use your memories of this guy to refuse to have anything to do with me."

Andrea hadn't realized it, but they had both leaned against the desktop until their faces were only inches apart, their gazes glaring.

She straightened, crossed her arms and took a deep breath.

"Robert was my father," she said matter-of-factly. "And he treated me the same way you've treated Denise. He flitted in and out of my life. Home long enough to decide what friends I should have, what schools I should attend, but never long enough to see if I was happy or if any of his plans came to fruition. And nothing, absolutely nothing, stood in the way of his never-ending search for fame and fortune, which came in the guise of that one grand-but-always-elusive business deal."

She saw Ian frown and her voice fell into a flat monotone as she continued, "And you, Ian Powers, are just like him. You can say you love your family all you want, you can make them all kinds of promises, promises you think you'll keep, but when that phone rings and that irresistible transaction is dangled in front of your face, you're going to be out of here. History. On the next plane to Seattle or Hong Kong or wherever."

Ian's frown deepened and he slowly nodded his head. "You've summed me up quite well, haven't you?" Then he added, "Especially for only having spent a total of twenty minutes with me yesterday."

"I think I have."

"Since you have things summed up so neat and tidy, I guess I'd be wasting my breath telling you that you're wrong. Granted, you did point out some weaknesses in my relationship with Denise. And I'm taking steps to correct them. I've arranged my schedule so that I can—"

"Look," Andrea interrupted, "nothing you can say is going to make me change my mind. I don't believe you could commit yourself to train for that run. And, even if you could, there's not enough time. Normal training for a half marathon would take six months, maybe longer. The Wilmington Challenge is in four. You'd need a tremendous amount of determination to train for a half marathon in that short a period of time."

"This is important to me," he stressed. "I can do this...."

But his voice died when he saw the clear finality in the quick shake of her head.

A knock on the door made them both turn toward it. Without waiting for a summons, Mr. Scott poked his head into the office.

"Miss O'Connor, do you realize that there are unsupervised children out on the track?"

"Yes, and I'm on my way," she said.

"It is not your job to be on your way," Mr. Scott pompously pointed out. "It's your job to be out there."

Andrea snatched up her clipboard and stopwatch. "I understand that, and I'm—"

"This is my fault," Ian said, pulling the door open wide so the principal could see him.

"Well, Mr. Powers, hello." Mr. Scott's tone changed so abruptly, Andrea rolled her eyes heavenward. "If you were having a problem," he said, "you should have come directly to me."

"As a matter of fact, I would like to speak to you if you have a moment." Ian stepped out into the hall, guiding Mr. Scott along with him. He closed the door, leaving Andrea alone in her office without so much as a farewell.

On her way out to the track, Andrea sucked air into her lungs and exhaled with force. "Ian Powers," she muttered, "you are bound and determined to get me fired."

Later that evening, Andrea stood in front of her closet, so angry she could barely breathe. She kicked off her royal-blue pumps and reached down to snatch them up.

"The man is infuriating!" She flung one shoe into the bottom of the closet, where it collided with several other neatly ordered pairs. The other shoe followed, its impact scattering shoes everywhere.

Gunther whimpered and tucking his tail between his legs, slunk out of the bedroom.

"How could that man think he could force me to do this?" Reaching around behind her, she struggled with the zipper of her yellow-and-blue striped shirt dress. "I won't do it! Ohhhh," she moaned when the zipper became stuck. "Damn you, Ian Powers!"

She yanked hard and was rewarded with the sound of ripping material. "Damn! Now look what he's made me do."

She pulled the dress off and sat on the edge of the bed to examine the small tear in the brightly colored fabric. Sighing deeply, she closed her eyes and let the aggravating scene play through her head. Mr. Scott might have been the one doing the urging, but Andrea knew without a doubt that Ian Powers was the instigator.

Having showered and changed after track practice, Andrea had stayed at school to grade tests. Mr. Scott's visit to her office had surprised her; he usually summoned teachers to his private domain if he wished to speak to them.

"I think I've found a way to provide that new track equipment you've been wanting," Mr. Scott had said.

"You have?" Andrea had been stunned. But, looking back on it, she should have been suspicious at his offer. Mr. Scott had never been a willing participant in a discussion about the much-needed equipment.

Andrea had dropped her red pen on top of the pile of test papers, her eyes narrowing. "You're not going to suggest that the kids raise that kind of money on their own, are you?"

"No. No, nothing like that," he'd assured. "This is a great idea. And not much work for you, either."

Andrea had looked at him, unable to restrain the dubious expression that crossed her face. Watching the principal strut toward her desk, she'd thought that all he needed to do was tuck his thumbs behind his suspenders to complete the look of utter pomposity.

"I do have to admit that I didn't come up with the idea all on my own. As you know, Ian Powers asked to speak to me this afternoon. Well, Ian—" Mr. Scott had looked down his nose at Andrea "—he invited me to call him Ian. Well, Ian told me he'd like to make a gift to the school. Something that the physical-education department might need."

Andrea had known immediately where the conversation was leading. She'd felt her shoulder muscles tighten and she'd pressed her lips together as the first stirrings of anger had surged through her.

"I told Ian of your desire to have some new equipment," Mr. Scott had continued, "but there's one little catch."

"Oh?" She'd raised one eyebrow, the only indication of her fury.

"Yes." Mr. Scott had looked uneasy, then he'd cleared his throat. "He would like to take just a little of your time to train for some race."

She should have known! Ian Powers had once again gone over her head to get what he wanted. Andrea had become uncontrollably livid. She'd stood so quickly that her chair had tipped backward and rammed against the wall.

"Did he happen to mention that I already refused to train him?" She'd stared, unperturbed, at Mr. Scott's astonishment.

"Umm . . . w-well . . ." he'd stammered.

"I told him that there wasn't enough time—"

"He told me," Mr. Scott broke in, "that you were being unreasonable. He told me you were angry that he'd tried to force you to put Denise back on the track team."

Andrea had glared at him. "No matter how generous *Ian's* offer is, it couldn't possibly cover the cost of the equipment I need."

"It's a very generous offer," Mr. Scott had informed her.

She'd ground her teeth and inhaled slowly, trying to regain her control.

"Look," the principal had said, his voice taking on an irritating quality of appeasement, "if you'll take the initiative to raise some of the needed funds on your own, then I'll see if I can get the school board to allocate your department something from the budget."

But when he'd witnessed the stubborn set of her jaw, Mr. Scott had raised his mulish chin to regal heights and stared down his nose at her. "You know that this school has been in need of new equipment for some time now," he'd stated, daring her to dispute. "And the means to get it is within your grasp. Ian Powers isn't asking for anything more than your time and expertise. I'm sure that you'll agree that it's your duty to this school and to your students to overcome any petty grudge you might be holding against this fine man. It's in your students' best interest that you do."

He'd then stomped out the door, leaving Andrea fuming.

Gunther's whine brought her back to the present. Andrea threw the torn dress on the bed and called the dog to her.

"I'm sorry I scared you," she crooned, smoothing the shepherd's soft brown coat. "It's just that I'm so mad at that man. He's infuriating!"

Gunther barked.

"I'm glad you agree." She smiled and patted his head. "What say we go out for a run? Maybe that will take my mind off all this."

Gunther barked twice in quick succession and ran for the door.

"Well, wait a minute, you big lug." Andrea laughed at the dog's exuberance. "I need to change. I can't run around town in my slip!"

The Wilmington skyline was silhouetted by a rosy haze as dusk enveloped the city. The evening breeze cooled Andrea's damp skin, and a quiet euphoria calmed her spirit. With Gunther close at her heels, she barely felt the pavement under her feet. She breathed deep and even, letting the sensation of "runner's high" wash over her.

All of the day's stress completely disappeared; her troubling thoughts melted away. Even though every muscle in her body was working to the limit, Andrea experienced a keen sense of relaxation. This was why she ran—this feeling of nirvana that few people ever experienced.

Turning onto Delaware Avenue, Andrea glanced at her watch and was surprised to see she'd been out for more than ninety minutes. She broke her stride to reach down and ruffle Gunther's fur.

"One more block, fella, and then we'll head for home."

They crossed the street and Andrea stopped short. Halfway up the block she saw Ian helping a statuesque brunette out of a car. The couple stood for a moment of conversation, and Andrea saw Ian's face light with laughter. All that could be seen of his date was a voluptuous cascade of dark hair, but Andrea knew by the admiration she read on Ian's face that the woman must be beautiful.

Andrea watched them enter a restaurant and suddenly all the tension and anger that she'd worked so hard to exorcise from her mind came flooding back to knot in her chest. She trotted on, passing the doors through which Ian and his date had disappeared.

"Who does he think he is?" she muttered. He was so damned smug. He knew she couldn't refuse to help him train if he offered the school that equipment. He was forcing her to help him.

When she reached the end of the block, she didn't turn toward home as she had promised Gunther. Instead, she turned right. And at the next corner she turned right again, circling the block of the restaurant where Ian was dining.

"I won't do it!" she said aloud. A man standing at the bus stop cast her a sidelong glance and she felt her cheeks flush.

But reality focused slowly, becoming crisper, more clear with each bouncing step. Her students needed that equipment. The equipment they had been forced to use was worn out, and Mr. Scott had no intention of purchasing new equipment. He'd stated that over and over.

She circled the block again. Damn it! She had to get that equipment for her students, her kids. And it looked as though training Ian Powers for the half marathon was the only way she was going to get it.

So, she decided, you have to give in. Her irritation raged inside her. But there's nothing that says I have to give in graciously!

She picked up her pace, racing around the corner and up the steps to the entrance to the restaurant.

"Sit. Stay," she ordered Gunther over her shoulder. The shepherd sat back on his haunches and watched his mistress enter the building.

Andrea brushed past the protesting maître d' and stopped inside the crowded room only long enough to scan the throng of people. Spotting Ian immediately, she marched toward the table where he sat with the gorgeous, raven-haired woman.

"So," Andrea announced, "you've gone over my head once again."

Ian jerked around to face her.

"Andrea!"

The astonishment contorting his features generated an immense satisfaction in Andrea.

She raised her eyebrows mockingly. "Don't twist my arm too far, though. It might break."

Ian bent to whisper something in his date's ear. Andrea's eyes traveled over the woman's cover-girl face, contoured cheeks, lushly mascaraed lashes, creamy red lips and she realized for the first time what she must look like—wilted running clothes, flat, damp hair, and lots of sweat-soaked skin.

Ian stood. "Let's go to the lobby and talk about this. It's really not like you think."

His placating tone and barely concealed smile struck a match to her embers of anger. Was he laughing at her?

"It's exactly like I think. And we don't need to go anywhere."

A number of patrons stopped eating and watched the scene with interest.

"Sir, should I escort the lady out?" The maître d' had come up behind Andrea.

"I'll handle it," Ian said over her shoulder.

Andrea pointedly ignored everyone but Ian.

"You want a coach, you've got a coach." She plucked the forgotten highball glass out of his hand. "But no more alcohol . . ." She picked up the lit cigarette resting in the ashtray on the table. "And no more smoking." She dropped it into the amber liquid in the glass. The cigarette sizzled and sputtered out. "Don't order beef, order fish. Grilled. I'll see you at the school in the morning, six o'clock sharp."

Turning on her heel, she walked out of the dining room and through the lobby.

"Andrea, wait," Ian called.

She stopped at the glass doors and swung around to face him.

"You told me I'd need a tremendous amount of determination to do this," he said. "I think I have what it takes."

Cocking her head dubiously, she placed her hand on her hip. "Well, we'll certainly see, won't we?"

"Come on, now. Don't be angry."

"How can you expect me not to be?" she asked. "You barge into my life and—"

"I know, I know." He took another step toward her, his gaze softening. "In spite of the situation, I do appreciate what you're doing."

Her lips curved into a slow, wicked grin. "Let's see if you can still say that after tomorrow's workout."

He came closer. "Ooo," he whispered, "that sounds ominous."

Andrea watched him reach out and then felt his fingers slide along her jaw, his skin cool and smooth on hers.

Her eyes narrowed, and she took a step back. "Take your hands off me or be prepared to experience an enormous amount of pain." She glared at him for a split second before turning and racing down the steps to the street. "Be on time," she ordered over her shoulder.

She whistled to Gunther, and the two of them ran off down the block.

"Hey!" Ian had stepped out the door to call after her, "You know what they say, no pain, no gain."

Chapter Four

How could she possibly have agreed to this? That question had rolled around in Andrea's brain all night. And it had been a night filled with restless dreams, dreams in which she found herself running from a looming, relentless shadow.

She leaned against the fence surrounding the school's track, slowly stretching her calf muscles, relishing the breeze that ruffled through her hair. The cool morning air helped to clear her mind.

Shaking her head, she wondered, yet again, how she had let herself be bullied into training Ian Powers to compete in the Wilmington Challenge.

He's a pushy, overbearing brute, she thought. He's the type of man she had purposefully stayed away from, the type of man who had a tendency to tell her when and where she would be doing what, with whom and how. Ian infuriated her. Each time she came into contact with him, she became angry.

Remembering their first meeting, Andrea closed her eyes and once again felt the electricity that had passed between them as they stood there in the hallway. It was strong and vibrant, as though it had a life of its own. And they hadn't even known each other. Then she remembered that, in spite of her anger, she'd experienced those same vibrations each time she'd been near him. She'd even felt them last night in the restaurant lobby. In fact, the magnetism had had such strength in its pull, she'd thought Ian had been about to lean toward her and place his lips on hers.

She opened her eyes and took a deep gulp of the crisp April air.

"That's absurd," she grumbled. How could he have wanted to kiss her when she had looked such a mess? Don't let your imagination get the best of you, she chided herself.

The voluptuous woman sitting with Ian last night came to mind. And Andrea also remembered, with a pang of regret, how she herself must have appeared, standing in that restaurant, scolding Ian. It wasn't a pretty picture.

The woman's model-perfect face certainly had been a contrast to her own shiny, perspiring one. The navy dress Ian's date had been wearing had set off the woman's luscious length of dark hair. Andrea's damp tank top and shorts had stuck to her body like a second skin, and tendrils of her hair had been glued to her face and neck.

Andrea's lips tilted in a rueful smile. She was now sure that she'd definitely been mistaken about Ian's move to kiss her.

She sat down on the grass and grasping her toes, gently pulled her body down over her outstretched legs. The steady pressure on her back and leg muscles felt wonderfully relaxing. And she knew she would need every bit of that relaxation if she was going to deal with Ian this morning.

Where was he anyway? she wondered. It wouldn't surprise her in the least if he didn't show up at all. It would take only one phone call offering some business deal or other to make him shuck all his plans of training. The thought irritated her.

Marveling at the range of emotions she could experience just thinking of the man, Andrea knitted her brow. She'd never reacted so strongly to another human being before. Except Robert. Her scowl deepened at the thought of her father, and she thrust it out of her mind.

She inhaled and bent one leg behind her to stretch out her thigh muscle. What was it about Ian Powers that made her want to dispute everything he did and said? He made her want to prove him wrong, do exactly the opposite of what he demanded. She didn't stop to analyze why. She only knew that he needed to be shown that not everyone would bend to his will. Granted, she was embroiled in this whole mess because she had given in to him. But it was for a good cause. She was doing this for her students. Besides, she had no intention of bending any further.

Smiling once more, she thought of all the fun she was going to have showing him that she, too, had a will of iron. Especially when it came to training. Her smile broadened.

"What's so funny?"

Ian's husky voice made her heart skip a beat. She glanced up to see him towering over her. Her stomach quivered with anticipation and she inadvertently placed her hand there. Everything about him was commanding: his voice, his stance, his physique. She had to fight the urge to get up and flee.

Why did he ruffle her so? The pertinent question was why did she let him? There was nothing that said she had to be his friend. She didn't even have to like him. He wanted something from her, and she wanted something from him. It was as simple as that. All she had to do was see that he finished the Wilmington Challenge four months from now, and then she could collect his money, the money that would buy some of the new equipment for the school. After that, she need never see him again.

Her gaze left his face to travel downward, lingering on his broad chest, then lowering further to take in his muscled legs and sneaker-clad feet. She couldn't help the smile that tugged at her lips.

"You are," she quipped lightly in answer.

"Me?" Ian spread his arms wide, looked down at his cutoffs and T-shirt, then looked back at Andrea. "What's wrong with me? I'm ready to run."

He could see by the look on her face that she wanted to laugh, but was holding back. She pointed to his shorts.

"Those were blue jeans once."

"Yes," he said. "I took the scissors to them this morning."

Her silky blond hair brushed against her face as she shook her head, and then she did laugh.

His lips thinned with irritation. He hadn't been sure what to expect from Andrea this morning. After last night's little tirade in the restaurant he thought she might still be angry. Her anger he could have handled; her ridicule he could not.

"These shorts—"

"And those shoes will never do," she interrupted.

Ian was incredulous. "What's wrong with these shoes?" His eyes dropped to his feet and he unconsciously wiggled his toes in the canvas sneakers. When he looked up at her, his eyes were narrowed. "You never said special attire was required. We're only going to jog a few laps anyway!"

"Is that what you think we're going to do?" Her voice rose an octave. "Jog a few laps?"

She was extremely aggravating, he thought, but her eyes were incredible when she was angry. They darkened to a crystalline blue, hardened to chips of wintery ice. A sudden thought flashed through his mind and he wondered how those icy eyes would look melted in the heat of passion. But her frigid tone killed the image he was conjuring.

"Listen, Ian, if you think running a few easy laps is going to get you into good enough shape to participate in a half marathon, then you have another think coming."

She turned from him, then twisted back around. "And don't use that word. I don't *jog*. I run." She turned again and took a few steps, mumbling, "I hate that word."

"Ah-h-h," Ian teased, "she doesn't jog. She runs."

Andrea whirled on him. "This isn't fun and games, Ian. It's a very serious subject to me. Nonrunners have contempt for people who run. They think runners are idiots with only two brain cells to rub together. Why else would we be pounding the pavement with grimaced faces?"

"Whoa, wait just a minute," Ian said, an indignant frown on his brow. "Come down off your high horse a minute. You make it sound as though every person who doesn't run has a low opinion of those who do. I, for one, respect those people out there 'pounding the pavement' as you call it. And my father would love to run, but he's not able to."

He watched all the anger drain from her as her cheeks flushed with embarrassment.

"I'm sorry. I didn't mean to preach." She brushed her hair back from her face, but the fine strands fell from her fingers to curl at her cheekbone as before. "It's just that I want you to know that training isn't easy. And if you want to do this, you're going to have to work hard every day for the next four months. Even then, you might not be ready."

"I understand all that." His voice was soft. "And I need for you to understand that I mean to do this. And I'm prepared to work hard."

"Okay." She smiled at him. "I guess we should get started."

"What about my shoes and clothes?"

"Go to the athletic shop in the mall today," she said. "Tell the salesperson that you want a training shoe. I'll warn you now that they're going to be expensive, but don't skimp. Your body will thank you for it."

She ignored his "harrumph."

"You can get some shorts there, too," she continued. "Buy something loose, unrestraining. Someone there can help you pick out a nice pair."

Glancing down at his high-tops, she giggled. "It looks as though you've had those for years. But hold on to them, they're coming back into style." She laughed again. "They'll have to do for today. You won't be able to do much at first anyway."

Won't be able to do much, she says. Ian gritted his teeth, refusing to comment. He'd just store that insult with all the rest she'd given him, way to the back of his mind. But, nevertheless, the insults rankled. Won't be able to do much. I'll show her, he thought. Just let him get her out on that track and he'd show her who wouldn't be able to do much.

As Andrea demonstrated a series of stretching exercises, Ian watched patiently, his eyes traveling over her firm body and sculptured legs. Her flexing and relaxing muscles mesmerized him. The skimpy running outfit she wore exposed so much of her creamy smooth skin. He became fascinated by how apparently physically fit she was. He couldn't understand how such an irritating woman could be so tantalizing.

"Ian?" His eyes snapped up to her face. "Are you paying attention?"

"Definitely." He fought the impulse to grin.

"I want you to be sure and stretch each muscle group before you run," she said. "At least ten minutes."

She stood and brushed off her bottom. Ian swallowed as he watched the movement against her silky shorts. Feeling his insides tighten, he wondered how such an innocent action could stir him so deeply.

"Now, you try." Her voice brought his eyes once more to her face.

He cleared his dry throat, then lowered himself to the ground, watching her long legs as he went.

"Like I said before," Andrea told him, "you won't be able to do much at first."

The warm desire he was feeling suddenly congealed to a thick angry determination. He could do more than she ever imagined, he decided. A firm resolve settled in his chest as he stretched the length of his torso over his straightened legs.

His muscles protested, burning with red-hot pinpoints of fire, but he ignored them and pressed himself down even farther.

"Don't bounce," Andrea warned. "What you want is a slow, steady pressure. Now, release."

Ian stifled his urge to groan.

"Now, again."

Clenching his teeth, Ian proceeded to reach toward his toes again.

"Legs straight," Andrea instructed. "Knees locked. Good. And relax."

After several sets of stretching and relaxing, she sat down beside him.

"Now, bend your left foot behind you. Like this."

Ian tried to contort his leg the way she was doing, but his knee didn't lay flat as hers did. His stuck up awkwardly, and the pain in his thigh was excruciating.

"Press your left knee toward the ground."

"You are kidding, right?" Ian growled.

Andrea smiled and shook her head. "Nope."

His back arched, and he grimaced at the effort. His knee didn't budge.

The sound of her laughter trickled over him, strengthening the stubbornness in his spirit.

"Don't be disappointed at how you're doing," Andrea told him. "You can't expect much when your muscles are out of shape."

Out of shape? He'd do this on willpower alone if he had to! He strained and pressed his knee toward the ground and was elated when it lowered a fraction of an inch.

"Now, the right," Andrea said, seemingly oblivious to his success.

Ian sighed with relief when he straightened and relaxed his left thigh muscle. But the pain started anew when he bent his right foot back behind him. His jaw muscle tensed, and he suffered through the exercise.

After twenty minutes of pulling, pushing and stretching, Ian was sure he'd used every muscle on his body because each one was screaming at him. His determination to prove to Andrea that he could do anything she instructed had foolishly led him to overexert. And her demands never diminished in the least—if anything, they increased.

A slow burning anger began to build in him. What did she think he was anyway? A sideshow contortionist? He knew she was trying to push him into crying uncle. And he was just as mulishly intent on showing her he wouldn't quit.

He once more found himself on the ground with his left leg bent to the side, his right extended.

"Lie back," Andrea insisted.

When he did, she ran an index finger down his left thigh and said, "See there, it's nice and limber now. Your knees are almost level. That's great."

The contact of her skin on his and the smug tone of her voice ignited a flame of irritation in him. It swirled and mingled with the determination and anger and desire already burning in the pit of his stomach, making him want to reach out and . . . and . . . what? Teach her a lesson? Prove himself a man? Beat her at her own game?

He didn't know. But the urge to snatch her to him, feel her against him was overpowering.

Andrea felt a little guilty for having pushed Ian so hard. He'd be sore tomorrow, she knew. She was crouched on the balls of her feet, her hand resting lightly on his knee when his fingers encircled her wrist, taking her completely off guard. His gentle tug overbalanced her and she tumbled across his chest. She felt his arms wreathe her waist and his fingers lock at the small of her back.

Shaking her hair out of her eyes, she looked into his face and glared. "What do you think you're doing?"

"I'm taking a break."

"With me on top of you?" she asked testily.

She saw his eyebrows raise a fraction and his eyes lit with mischief.

"That bothers you?"

Her glare narrowed. "As a matter of fact, it does."

"Well, by all means, let's fix that."

He twisted his body and rolled until he was on top, looming over her, his hands still nestled at her back.

"Better?"

"Ian!" Her eyes went wide as she protested angrily, "I'm not a teenager. And I don't find rolling in the grass all that exciting." But the warm pressure of him made her heart beat erratically in her chest. Her breath started coming in gasps. She swallowed nervously and felt a tremendous need to hide her reaction to his nearness.

"Let me up." She tried to pull her arms free from where he had them pinned to her sides.

"But I've been such a good boy," he whispered, turning a blind eye to her squirming. "Don't you think I deserve a reward?"

His voice was like warm velvet, and she felt a heated desire swell inside her. She swallowed again and ground her teeth, determined that he wouldn't see the effect he was having on her.

"Then, I'll get you a lollipop or something later," she spat out, struggling with renewed strength. "Let me up!"

"A lollipop? But I'd much rather taste the sweetness of your lips."

Ian's intimate words caressed her. Her blood rushed through her veins like liquid fire, heating every part of her. A giddy excitement slowly churned inside her, building itself to a crazy speed, but through the flustered haze her mind fought for control.

"You wouldn't dare!" She fixed him with a stormy stare, as her will to fight battled with the desire building inside her. "Ian," she warned.

But he ignored her.

He leaned even closer. She could feel his breath graze her cheek. "Ian." Her voice sounded weaker this time.

Again, he ignored her. "I can see your pulse pounding," he said. "Here." He placed warm lips against her temple where a delicate vein betrayed her. "And here." His mouth moved to the silky hollow of her throat.

"Ian." She whispered his name with a plea, but whether she meant for him to stop or continue she couldn't tell.

When he covered her lips with his, she stopped fighting and gave herself over to the sensations his gentle, searching kiss created in her body. She felt light and warm. The heat that radiated through every fiber centered in the core of her being, beating a throbbing rhythm there.

The urge to arch her back against him was strong, and when she gave in to it, he deepened the kiss. His tongue petitioned entrance into her mouth and she opened it to his passionate exploration.

Her mind began to spin until there were no thoughts at all. The only things in existence were his mouth on her mouth, his body pressing against her body and the desire that this should never end. But it did.

When Ian lifted his head, Andrea lay there with her eyes closed, feeling her heart slow its racing. She opened her eyes slowly, reluctantly. After she did, she wished she hadn't.

The grin on Ian's face couldn't have been wider.

"Andrea, that was great."

"Oh, God," she groaned. His grip on her had relaxed, so she pulled one hand free and covered her eyes.

"I can't believe how your body was talking to me." He teased her with his brash tone and a cocky lifting of his eyebrow.

But Andrea didn't find it amusing. Biting back a curse, she planted her palm against his jaw and shoved him off of her. She whipped herself to her feet and turned toward the track, calling to him over her shoulder.

"It's time for *your* body to do some talking. See if you can keep up."

Andrea ran off at a swifter pace than she knew he could match, at least not for any length of time. She wasn't just angry, she was livid. Part of her anger was focused on Ian, and she needed to get away from him, fast. But most of her fury was directed at herself.

Why did she react to him the way she did? She was an adult, wasn't she? Why couldn't she control her emotions? Why couldn't she control her own body's response to that man?

At the first turn on the track, she glanced over her shoulder to see Ian trying to catch up with her. She lengthened her stride, desperate to put as much space between them as possible. When she was a half lap ahead of him, she slowed down just enough to keep the distance between them. She knew she should be running with him, coaching him, encouraging him, but she couldn't bring herself to do that, not right now.

As she ran, she kept looking over to her left toward Ian, trying to figure out what it was about him that made her forget all the promises she'd made to herself about staying away from domineering men. Pushy men. Overbearing men. Men like her father. Men like Ian.

She lapped the track again.

Why did she want him? She did want him. She had to admit that to herself. She'd wanted him from day one. Granted, he was handsome. Okay, gorgeous. With his dark eyes and hair and those wide, strong shoulders, any woman would say he was good-looking. But his character was everything she despised. Bossy. Arrogant. Aggressive.

What was wrong with her? Forget him, she commanded herself. Pushing him from her mind, she trotted on, trying to relax and enjoy the run.

The sun warmed her skin and she lifted her face to it. Birds were singing cheerily, and the fragrance of spring blooms was in the air, but it was impossible to find any pleasure when she was wrapped in such a thick blanket of emotion.

Andrea rounded a turn and realizing she was halfway through her seventh lap, she glanced to her left. She slowed her pace when she didn't see Ian. Frightened, she stopped and scanned the grounds. She saw him lying flat on his back on the other side of the track. Dashing across the fifty-yard line of the football field, Andrea headed straight toward him.

She frowned when she saw his chest heaving. And when she knelt down beside him, he moaned.

"Ian?"

"I'm going to die."

Relief flooded through her. She'd thought he was hurt.

"Get up," she commanded.

"I'm going to die," he groaned louder.

"No, you're not." She tugged at his arm. "Come on, get up and walk it off or you'll start to cramp up."

"Just let me lie here and die."

"Ian, get up," she demanded, pulling harder.

She helped him to his feet, and he leaned on her heavily. They walked several steps before either of them spoke. He started to cough and gasp for breath. When his fit was over, he groaned.

"Ian." Andrea couldn't help laughing. "You didn't even run long enough to work up a sweat."

"Good," he murmured, "then I won't smell bad at my funeral."

"There won't be any funeral," she said emphatically. "You'll be fine after a cool down."

Ian acted as though he hadn't heard her as he asked, "You'll say something nice at my eulogy, won't you?"

"Ian!" Andrea laughed again. "Okay, okay. I'll be sure and tell everyone that I was very impressed with the deceased."

"You were?" Ian stopped leaning on her and turned a curious eye her way.

"Umm-hmm." She nodded. "I expected you to finish two, maybe three laps. You ran six. Ian, that's a mile and a half. You're darned straight I'm impressed."

Andrea watched as a cocky smile tilted one side of Ian's mouth, and suddenly he had more pep in his step.

"So, you were impressed," he said.

Soon he was downright swaggering, his lips pulled tight with an arrogant grin, and Andrea was sorry she complimented him at all.

"I see you're feeling better all ready," she commented dryly.

"As a matter of fact, I am. You were impressed."

Andrea rolled her eyes and shook her head. She thought of how he'd feel tomorrow and grinned, slow and wide.

"Well, remember how you're feeling right now," she advised, "because you're going to be sore in the morning."

"Oh, I can handle a little soreness," he said, confidence evident in the lift of his shoulders.

"You're going to have a lot of lactic acid built up in your muscles."

"Lactic what?" he asked, turning to face her.

"Acid. Your muscles convert carbohydrates to energy," she explained, "and one of the by-products that's given off is lactic acid. That's one of the reasons muscles feel sore."

"And, like I said—" Ian sauntered up the hill toward the parking lot "—I can handle a little soreness. Just remember what you said. You were impressed."

Andrea sighed patiently.

"Same time tomorrow?" he asked, sticking a key in the lock of his car door.

She nodded.

"Tomorrow I'm going to knock your socks off." He gave a cocksure laugh and revved the car engine.

She watched him drive off before turning toward the school's gymnasium entrance. Ian didn't realize how painful his muscles were going to be. He had overworked his body trying to prove himself. She really should feel bad about prodding him to run so far his first time out. But he'd deserved it—kissing her like that.

Boy, she thought, is he going to be hurting tomorrow. She couldn't help laughing out loud.

Chapter Five

Andrea stood on the grass at one end of the asphalt track and shielding her eyes from the morning sun, looked up at the spectators filling the stands. It was the largest crowd ever to come watch the Highland Striders compete in a track meet. Many of the people waved flags or shakers that were blue and yellow, the Highland Academy colors. Andrea also saw blue-and-yellow caps and T-shirts, balloons and streamers, among other things, that showed school spirit and support for the team. Two teams toted a large sign that read Go Highland!

Swiveling her head, Andrea saw that the bleachers on the opposite side of the track were also filling up. And she could easily see from the opposing team's fans that their school's colors were red and black. This meet was going to be an exciting one with two such competitive schools vying for a place in the state championships.

There couldn't have been a more beautiful Saturday to hold a meet. Andrea let her eyes rove over to where her team's members were stretching together, rallying one another with teasing hoots and cheers, rousing a high level of competitiveness. She didn't mind the kids carrying on and didn't fight the broad smile that came to her lips. There was a time for serious training and there was a time to flaunt your stuff. She knew the Striders had worked hard and now it was time for them to show what they could do.

She ran over to join in the fun, knowing that her participation would motivate the runners and give them the confidence to run harder, throw longer and jump higher.

Weaving through the stretching bodies, Andrea stopped to give quick words of encouragement and last-minute tips. The sight of Denise bending over straight legs brought an intense thought of Ian, and Andrea's eyes immediately scanned the crowd.

As she looked for him, her heart beat a fierce rhythm and she remembered the times they'd spent together over the past four weeks.

Every day she had expected him to give up or just not show up. But Ian had surprised her, sticking to the schedule she'd made for him. Knowing how difficult his training had been, she'd had to admit that he'd proved his determination.

Andrea had been so sure he would give up after that first workout. Her lips tightened against the smile the images of that next day brought: the way he'd hobbled onto the track, his groans while stretching out his sore muscles and his curses while running. But he had run, that day and every day.

She thought about the kiss he'd forced on her. She'd been furious with him, so furious that as soon as she'd escaped him, she'd flown around the track as though she'd had wings, expecting Ian to do the same and unmindful that to do so might cause him injury.

She'd been more angry with herself than she had been with him. Because she'd reveled in the feel of his lips on hers, savored the taste of him. So much so that she'd forgotten the promise that she'd made to herself not to become involved with him.

Determined that she wouldn't forget again, she'd fortified her resolve to avoid personal involvement with him enough so that when he'd tried to kiss her again, she'd threatened to cut the thin business thread that bound them by ending their training sessions. After that, he'd kept a respectful distance.

But over the four weeks that they'd been training together, Andrea couldn't ignore the jarring undercurrent that constantly pulsated between them. It was like being in a summer storm in which no rain fell— only an endless supply of thunder and lightning.

She tried hard to ignore the electricity she felt when she was with Ian. She tried to remember all the things about him she didn't like: his bossy overbearing manner, his arrogance and stubbornness. But as she'd spent more and more time with him, she had come to know him, whether she'd wanted to or not. And as hard as she'd tried not to like him, she'd finally confessed to herself that he *did* have a few good qualities.

Ian loved his family. Andrea knew that he was spending a great deal of time with Denise lately. And he'd arranged his schedule so that he could train for the half marathon, knowing that this was something that would make his father happy.

During the last month, Andrea's common sense battled unceasingly with her instinct. She didn't know why, but she wanted him to be good and kind, and she was coming to believe he was.

But deep down inside she knew he couldn't help but revert back to the conquering, single-minded businessman he had been when she'd first met him. The kind of man she wouldn't let herself become involved with. His eagerness to improve his family relationships was only a phase. A phase he would soon grow tired of. A phase she must keep to the forefront of her mind at all times.

If she didn't, she might easily fall under his spell....

"He's not here."

Denise's miserable voice snapped Andrea back to the present. Kneeling down on one knee, Andrea rested her arms on her thigh. The look in the teen's sad eyes told her Denise could only be referring to Ian.

"You told him you were back on the team?" Andrea asked softly.

Denise only nodded, and Andrea could see she was fighting tears.

"And he said he would come?"

Denise's silent answer was to gaze once again at the bleachers, searching in earnest for a glimpse of her father.

The girl's expression of disappointment brought a myriad of emotions bubbling up in Andrea's chest so bitter she could taste them. Time and again she had suffered the same disillusionment sparked by her own father.

"Are you angry?" Denise made an effort to swallow around the question.

Andrea's brow knitted. "Why would I be angry?"

"At Dad," Denise said, "for not showing up this morning to run."

Shaking her head, Andrea said, "We weren't scheduled to run today. I wanted him to take a day off because we're going to increase mileage tomorrow. It'll be our first long run. Four miles."

"Well, don't be surprised if he doesn't show."

Denise's words were biting, and the girl bent over her legs, letting her hair fall across her face. Andrea heard her sniff.

Before Andrea could say anything, Denise explained, "He flew to Connecticut yesterday afternoon. There was some emergency. That's what he told Pops, anyway. I didn't get a chance to see him before he left." Denise wiped the back of her hand across her eyes. "He told Pops to tell me he'd be back in time to see me run today, but he's not coming. I just know it."

Andrea knew from personal experience that phrases like "maybe he'll be late" or "he's on his way" weren't a bit of help to a child who had been let down over and over again. So Andrea did the only other thing available. She tried to change the subject.

"How do you feel?" She touched Denise's sleeve to get her attention and smiled at her. "Are you ready to run the fastest mile of the day? The rest of the team looks raring to go."

Andrea knew she was prattling, but she also knew that the best way to help Denise was to distract her thoughts away from her father.

"Yeah," Denise said sullenly.

Andrea looked up at the crowd.

"And your grandfather's here." She emphasized her statement with a bright tone.

Denise lifted her head to look in her grandfather's direction, a hint of a smile tilting her lips.

"He wouldn't miss my running for the world."

"And neither would I," Andrea expressed. "Listen, promise me you'll introduce me to your grandfather before you leave today."

"Sure." Denise was smiling in earnest now.

Andrea stood and brushed at a piece of grass that clung to her knee. "I need to make sure the sprinters are setting up their starting blocks. The meet's about to begin." She turned to go, and Denise's voice called her back.

"Thanks, Miss O'Connor."

Andrea smiled in answer, but as she made her way over to where the team's fastest runners were setting up blocks on the starting line, she was filled with a deep gloom and her heart began to ache.

She knew it was coming. She knew the real Ian was going to reappear. Hadn't she just finished lecturing herself about this very subject? Why, then, was she so disturbed? Why was she feeling this profound sense of loss?

Swallowing the knot that had formed in her throat, Andrea pushed all thoughts of Ian from her mind. Her kids needed her. She didn't have the time to be distressed over promises that Ian had made and not fulfilled. But she couldn't help the rancor that froze in her chest like a chunk of ice, armoring her against the next time she faced him.

About halfway through the meet, Andrea was studying her clipboard, checking and rechecking the Strider's times and scores. She was pleased by their excellent performance and by the fact that they had a slight lead on the other team.

"Miss O'Connor!"

Andrea turned at the sound of Denise's shout to see her standing by her grandfather, whose wheelchair she'd pushed through the gate and onto the grass.

The older man looked sour, but Andrea smiled at him anyway and said, "Hello."

"Pops," Denise introduced, "this is my coach, Miss O'Connor. Miss O'Connor, my pops, Harry Powers."

"It's nice to meet you, Mr.—"

"It's Harry," he barked. "You're the one who threw my granddaughter off the track team." His tone was crotchety and accusing.

"Excuse him," Denise said to Andrea, ignoring her grandfather's moodiness. "He's not as bad as he makes himself out to be." To her grandfather she pointed out, "She's also the one who put me back on the team *and* she's training me for the Wilmington Challenge, so be nice."

"Yes, well . . ." Harry Powers relented reluctantly.

Andrea couldn't help the fond smile that came to her lips, seeing the affectionate relationship these two shared.

"Pops told me just this morning how happy he was that you were helping me and Dad."

"I'm delighted that I can help," Andrea said. "You're an enthusiastic runner. And your dad isn't so bad, either." She chuckled, but instantly regretted her last statement when she saw the shadow that crossed Denise's face.

"I'm proud of them," Harry said, clasping Denise's hand. "And I'm glad they have someone who knows running to help them along."

Andrea could tell that praise was not something that Harry Powers doled out indiscriminately, so she was honored by the veiled compliment.

"Denise told me how you won the first Wilmington Challenge," Andrea said to Harry. "You must have been very good."

Harry visibly drew into himself, as though for protection, but commented, "Better than some, not as good as others."

"Then you could have trained Denise and Ian yourself," Andrea said.

Denise's breath sucked in, and Harry lifted his chin to eye Andrea severely.

"I can't do anything with these crippled legs."

"You don't need to use your legs to coach," Andrea stressed. "Just your knowledge of the sport, your wit and your voice. You certainly have all of those."

His eyes narrowed, and his mouth turned down in a frown. He looked at her a moment before speaking. "I know enough about running to know that your sprinters could have taken first place if they'd kept their bodies low out of the blocks rather than snapping themselves erect at the sound of the gun."

So he was going to retaliate and show his disapproval at her suggestion by attacking her coaching abilities. That was okay with her, she thought, smiling easily. She was confident in her competence as a teacher and coach.

"You know, I've worked with these kids over and over on that very point and I just can't get them to understand that the starting blocks are pointless if they're not going to be used properly." Focusing all her attention on his face, she asked, "What do you suggest?"

"You don't want an old man's opinion."

"You're not so old, and I certainly do," she said. "I'd like some advice."

"Well, remember that advice is free and you can take it or not," Harry stated dourly. "But I think you should line your sprinters up in the starting blocks and have two people string a line across the track about waist high and four yards in front of them. Have them practice starting with the idea of staying low enough to clear the line. Their momentum alone will take at least a full second off their best times."

Andrea noticed that as Harry let himself get caught up in talking about running, his face transformed. His narrowed eyes and glowering expression brightened considerably. And even though the look couldn't be called smiling, it was definitely more affable.

"You know, you should come to track practice after school and give the kids some pointers." Andrea could see that Harry loved the sport of running, but still she fought the impulse to step back in anticipation of the response her suggestion would bring.

An excited uproar from the crowd made Andrea turn her head toward the track just in time to see one of her hurdlers catch her knee on a metal hurdle and skid to the ground, grazing knees, palms and chin in the process.

Calling a hurried "Excuse me" to Denise and her grandfather, Andrea sprinted toward the injured runner. After discovering that, other than a few scratches, the girl's pride was what had been injured most, Andrea asked if she wanted to finish the race.

"But I'll take last place." The disheartened teen swiped at her eyes and sniffed loudly.

"Yes, but last place is better than no place," Andrea encouraged her. "And it's the best way to show them that you're not licked."

The girl smiled with trembling lips and trotted off down the lane, jumping the hurdles slowly, but perfectly. She finished amidst a fury of applause from the stand of spectators.

Andrea didn't have a chance to think about Harry Powers again until she called Denise to get ready for the eight-eighty relay race. Denise was running the first leg, and Andrea wanted all four runners to take a quick practice at handing off the baton. They had performed the skill flawlessly at track practice yesterday, but Andrea knew more practice could only make them better.

"You really got to Pops when you told him he should come to practice," Denise said while they waited for the others to spread out across an open piece of ground.

Andrea pressed her lips together with remorse and nodded. "I know and I'm sorry. I shouldn't have opened my mouth like that."

"Don't be sorry." Denise grinned. "I've wanted to say those very things to him a hundred times, but I didn't have the guts."

"Well, it didn't help any if all it did was make him angry."

Denise shrugged. "He'll get over it. And maybe it'll make him think. I know he'd be happier if he were involved with running in some way."

"You're pretty smart, you know that?" Andrea asked, tugging on Denise's pony tail. "Now, let's see you hand off that baton as beautifully as you did yesterday."

The four runners' perfect timing in the delivery of the baton to one another during the relay race helped in their victory. The team took first place and pushed the Striders that much more ahead of the other team. The four girls were panting but exuberant with their win.

Andrea spent the next hour supervising field events: the long jumps, high jump and discus throw. Even though she was kept fully occupied, thoughts of Ian chiseled into her mind and she found herself glancing repeatedly toward the bleachers.

She hoped he would come. For Denise's sake, of course. Anxiety began to build inside her. An anxiety she hadn't felt since she was a teenager, hoping for, craving her father's presence at some function or other.

What are you doing? she asked herself. How could she be so gullible? Ian wasn't going to show up. Just like her father had never shown up. Ian was who he was, a business man with a one-track mind, and she couldn't change that.

It made her furious to think that Ian could stir those painful memories that she'd buried deep. She couldn't believe she was looking for him. But still she kept glancing toward the gate.

The mile run, the last event of the day, was getting closer. Andrea could see Denise becoming more agitated by the minute. She once again walked up to the parking lot looking for her father. Andrea was becoming more and more angry with Ian. How could a parent do this to his child?

"Ian shouldn't have promised her he'd come," Andrea told Harry as she watched Denise go out through the gate and jog up the grassy slope toward the lot.

"It must have been something important to keep him away," Harry said.

"I guess you're right." But Andrea's voice held an edge. She'd made the statement only to be polite. Inside she fumed, remembering the hundreds of times that very excuse was given to her by well-meaning people as a justification for her own father's absence.

Andrea knew those excuses, even though born out of the best intentions, wouldn't help Denise. Just like they had never helped her. Denise needed to clear her mind and concentrate entirely on running her race. Andrea knew that was the only way the girl would get over feeling dejected.

"Denise," Andrea called, meeting the sullen teenager halfway from the parking lot.

"He's not coming."

"Look, you've got to forget about that right now," Andrea stressed. "It's time for you to run your mile. Are you up for it?"

Denise nodded solemnly.

They hustled back to the track as the runners were called to take their marks.

"I want you to focus on the track in front of you." Andrea squeezed her shoulder. "You can win this if you put your mind to it."

"I'll try," Denise said.

The gun went off and Andrea called, "Be tough!"

As the runners rounded the first lap of the race, some of them began to straggle behind the rest. Denise wasn't in the lead, but she was staying with the head pack and Andrea knew she was saving her strength for the final and toughest lap.

Three of the competitors dropped out during the third lap and as the remaining runners went into the fourth, Andrea watched as Denise lengthened her stride. She passed into second place and in the last quarter lap, she passed the leader, crossing the finish line the winner.

Andrea heard the crowd yelling for her and realized that her voice was loudest of all. The Striders gathered around Denise, clapping her on the back and cheering. Harry Powers looked proud enough to cry, his craggy face lighting with a huge smile.

"You did it," Andrea hollered above the others' voices as she made her way through the press of bodies toward Denise.

"I can't believe it," Denise panted.

"I knew you could do it!"

"So did I!" Harry had wheeled himself beside his granddaughter.

"Pops!" Denise threw her arms around the old man. "Thanks for being here." Pulling back to look at him, she suddenly burst into tears before running off toward the locker room.

"What's with Denise?" The girl who had skinned her chin looked up at Andrea with curious eyes.

"She'll be all right," Harry proclaimed gruffly. "She's just overexcited." He turned his chair and started toward the parking lot.

"She'll be okay," Andrea assured the concerned team members. But she wondered if she was telling them the truth.

"Denise," Andrea called as she pushed open the locker-room door. She'd tried to plan what to say in the short time it took her to walk up to the building, but she was afraid that no words she could prepare would make Denise feel any better.

"I'm in here."

Andrea rounded the corner into the rest room and found Denise staring, red eyed, into the mirror. When Denise saw her coach, fresh tears fell down her cheeks.

"Why didn't he come?"

Silently, Andrea enfolded Denise in her arms and hugged her tight.

"If he loved me, he'd be here." Denise's voice was muffled against Andrea's shoulder.

Andrea sighed deeply, fighting tears of her own.

"I don't know why he didn't come," she said softly. "But I've spent the last four weeks getting to know your dad and I do know one thing—" Andrea tipped up Denise's chin so their eyes met "—he loves you, Denise. Very much."

After Denise calmed down, the two of them sat on the wooden bench in the locker room.

"It wasn't always like this," Denise explained. "We used to be a real family. We used to be so close." She blew her nose on a tissue. "But after Mom died, everything changed. Pops came to live with us, and all Dad did was work."

"Maybe your mother's death was hard on him and his work was cathartic."

"But it's been years. *Years.*"

Having been there herself, Andrea knew there was no excuse good enough for a child in Denise's place, but for some unknown reason she had this overwhelming urge to try to explain Ian's behavior.

"I know, honey, but he's your father and he wants to give you everything he can, everything he thinks you need. So he has to work." Guilt, thick and heavy, washed over Andrea as the words left her mouth. She, too, felt Ian should have attended the meet today, and here she was giving Denise the very excuses she'd hated to hear as a child.

"But I need *him.*"

"I know. I know." Andrea shook her head. "It's hard to be a single parent. It's almost impossible to be the provider and caretaker both at the same time." She ran a hand down Denise's silky ponytail. "That's why you have your grandfather."

"Yeah, Pops loves me."

"Denise," Andrea chided mildly, "your father loves you, too."

"I know that. But I get so disappointed, and then I feel angry and I know I shouldn't."

"I understand." Andrea's tone was consoling. "It's tough being a kid these days."

Denise sighed.

"That was a fantastic run," Andrea said. "It won the track meet for us."

Chuckling, Denise said, "I didn't know that. I must have done all right."

Dropping her hands to her lap, Andrea asked, "You okay now?"

Denise nodded and smiled. "Thanks for talking to me."

Andrea held the door open for Denise to pass. "Wait. I've wanted to ask how the painting is going."

Denise's expression brightened. "It's great. The studio is terrific. I'm painting Pops something special."

"I'd love to see it," Andrea said. "When it's finished, maybe you'll bring it in?"

"Sure."

As Andrea watched Denise walk to the special van that enabled her grandfather to drive, her mind was cluttered with a multitude of emotions. She felt sorry for Denise. She was aggravated by the reticence Harry showed when Denise had burst into tears. But most of all, she was angry with Ian.

He'd forced her to lie to Denise, and she planned to let him know exactly how she felt about that. She'd see him tomorrow morning. *If* he showed up.

Sunday afternoon Andrea found herself weeding the flower border in the backyard. She'd never been more depressed than she was today. She'd waited for Ian this morning and he never showed up. She had known he wouldn't. Why, then, was she so disappointed?

She chopped at the weeds with a vengeance. Gunther nuzzled her with his cold wet nose and dropped a slimy tennis ball beside her. She picked it up with gloved fingers and heaved it.

"Go get it, boy."

Gunther bounded after the ball, and Andrea turned back to mutilating the weeds.

After several well-aimed jabs at the unwanted plants, she sighed and sat back on heels. It was warm for May, and she swiped at her forehead with the back of one hand. She sighed again and remembered this morning's run.

She'd waited thirty minutes past the time she and Ian had arranged to meet before setting out without him. Despite the beautiful day and Gunther's company, it was the most desolate and lonely run she'd ever experienced.

Even now she felt covered with a cloud of isolation. She spent a great deal of time alone and never had she been bothered by solitude. In fact, she enjoyed it.

It wasn't until Gunther whined that she realized he'd brought his ball back and had dropped it into her lap to be thrown again. She tossed it and stood, removing her work gloves and dusting off her trousers.

She went into the kitchen and soaped her hands under warm water at the sink. She didn't feel angry at Ian any longer. She was just disappointed with him.

What was so important that would make Ian miss the track meet that he'd promised Denise he'd attend? Important enough for him to miss their scheduled run? Did he plan on continuing his training? If so, when?

The questions rolled around in Andrea's head until she thought she would scream. She wished he were here right now so she could vent some of her frustration at the source.

Drying her hands, she thought about how nice it would be to get a few answers to her questions. And slowly her anger returned.

Good, she thought, her eyes narrowing dangerously. She could deal much better with anger than she could with this hollow emptiness she'd been feeling. And she couldn't wait to see Ian!

At that moment, the front doorbell chimed.

Chapter Six

Andrea crossed through the living room, still clutching the tea towel she'd used to dry her hands, and pulled open the door.

Ian. His name rang loudly in her mind, but she was momentarily shocked speechless at the sight of him. She'd been thinking about him so intensely all weekend, she wondered if she'd conjured his image.

Immediately she was assaulted by his raw sensuality, the sensuality she had vowed to ignore. It was hard to shun something so powerful, so distinct. Especially when he looked so good standing there in his shorts and casual cotton pullover. But then he'd look good in anything, she thought. Or nothing.

That shocking reflection snapped her out of the intimate vision that had popped into her head, and she stared at an obviously amused Ian. It annoyed her that he seemed to constantly read her thoughts, perceive her longing.

It's your imagination, she scolded herself.

Placing one hand on her hip and one on the doorknob, she tilted her head and glared. The twinkling in his eyes vanished and he shifted his weight from one foot to the other. He pulled one arm from behind him and offered her a bundle of fresh-cut tulips.

"A peace offering," he said.

She silently took the flowers from him, fingering their delicate petals, but when she lifted her gaze, her eyes were still ice cold.

"Come on, Andrea. Let me come in. We need to talk."

"You wouldn't survive a conversation with me right now," she informed him before stepping back and flinging the door closed.

As she turned and headed for the kitchen, she heard Ian stop the door from shutting completely by sticking his foot in its path.

"Ow!" he yelled. He shoved the door open and was hot on her heels in an instant.

"What is it with you?" he asked, following her into the kitchen.

Andrea ignored him, reaching into the cabinet under the sink and pulling out a white milk-glass vase.

"Andrea." Ian crouched down beside her.

Andrea stood and flipped on the tap, filling the vase with water.

Ian heaved a sigh and lifted himself up from where he'd been squatting.

Using his index finger, he brushed at a strand of her hair that was clinging to her jaw.

"Talk to me," he coaxed.

Still refusing to acknowledge his presence, Andrea began to arrange the bright tulips in the hobnailed vase.

"There's no use in trying to hide it," he said silkily. "I know you're angry."

"Ian..." Falling for his teasing lure like a trout swallowing a baited hook, Andrea pushed his caressing hand away. "*Angry* doesn't even begin to describe the way I feel." She moved the vase of flowers over to the table, amazed at how steady her hands were when her insides were trembling so violently.

She was hit with a rush of emotion—from relief that Ian was back, to disappointment at his lack of commitment to the training; from sheer pleasure at seeing him, to fury that he'd expected a puny bouquet of flowers to exonerate him.

"I've come to explain—"

"Just save your explanation," Andrea interrupted. "Go bare your soul to your daughter, she's the one who needs to hear your excuses."

"I've apologized to Denise," he said quietly.

"And she's forgiven you?"

He nodded.

"Well, I'm not a gullible, sweet-tempered sixteen-year-old."

"You can say that again." Ian's words were weighted with sarcasm.

Andrea glowered at him. "And what is that supposed to mean?"

Ian shrugged and grinned. "That you're certainly not sweet-tempered today."

"How can you expect me to be?" Andrea pulled out a kitchen chair with force and sat down. "You committed yourself to train for the Wilmington Challenge. You literally forced me to coach you. And after four solid weeks of hard work, you just decide not to show up one day. An important day! A day we were scheduled to increase mileage."

"Andrea, I had to go—"

"What?" she interrupted again. "Did you get wind of a business you could buy for a song?"

"It was a little—"

"Some poor bankrupt store owner who had no other choice but to sell?" Her voice rose, and she felt herself losing control.

"If you'll let me explain." He pulled a chair close to her, sat down and took her hands in his.

Andrea wasn't aware of the tears that spilled down her cheeks as she dug into her memory, thinking of the hundred and one excuses her father had given her for his absences and failings. He'd never been there when she needed him. Never. And now Ian was doing the same thing.

"Andrea, I can't believe you're so upset." Ian's fingers slowly rubbed her wrist. "I didn't completely ignore my training. I ran this morning before I caught the plane home. I even added a mile."

She sniffed and then breathed deeply, feeling numb and barely hearing his words.

"Denise was so disappointed," she mumbled. "There were so many times that I felt the same way when I was her age." She shook her head. "Every time I expected my father to show up, he never did." She'd been gazing off, but now looked into his eyes. "Ian, you shouldn't do that to Denise. It hurts too much."

Ian wrapped her in his arms and pulled her tight against his chest, realizing there was more to this than just his being away over the weekend. She wasn't just talking about Denise being hurt. She was talking about her own raw memories. Andrea must have experienced tremendous pain because of her father, and that infuriated him. It angered him further to think he had done something that would cause her to relive it all. The urge to protect her was strong and he tightened his embrace, resting his cheek on her silky hair.

He waited, hoping she would open up and talk to him, tell him about the memories that hurt her so. After several silent seconds he asked, "Want to talk about him? Your father, I mean."

She didn't respond.

"Do you ever see him now? Talk to him?"

"He sends a card on my birthday." Her comment was faint, as though her thoughts were still miles away. But her voice quickly grew strong. "No, I don't ever see him or speak to him." She tried to shrug out of the embrace. "And I'd rather not discuss him."

Ian opened his mouth to speak, to tell her that he thought she should have some sort of relationship with the man who was her father, but sensing Andrea's turmoil concerning the situation, he remained silent. He'd let it rest. If she wasn't ready to open up to him, he'd wait until she was.

He leaned back and tipped her chin up so he could look into her eyes. "I want you to let me explain why I stayed away longer than I'd planned."

Her eyes were clouded over and he was sure she wasn't fully attentive, but he continued anyway.

"There was a fire in a plant I'm part owner of in Connecticut. Several workers were badly burned. I stayed the extra day making sure that the families involved had everything they needed." Ian inhaled deeply. His frustration over the accident was still just below the surface and highly volatile.

"I'll have to go back in a few days, but I won't stay any longer than what's absolutely necessary."

He felt her hand cover his, her grasp warm and reassuring. Her eyes were clear and he knew she was once more there with him; no shadows of her memories remained.

"Of course, you had to stay," she whispered. "I'm sorry I made such a fuss." She stood and moved to stare out of the kitchen window.

"It's okay." Ian grinned. "That's what I like about you. You dive into things headfirst."

"The only trouble is," she said dryly, "I don't stop to check how deep the water is. One of these days I'm going to break my neck."

She turned again to gaze out the window where Gunther romped in the backyard. She hugged herself tightly, holding off a shiver. She'd almost poured out her heart to him. That would have been a terrible mistake. Once she let down her defenses, she didn't know if she'd be strong enough to raise them again.

You've got to keep things on an impersonal plane, she told herself. Don't let him in. Once he's in, you'll be lost against the desire you feel for him.

When she had told Ian that he had no other choice but to stay where he was needed, she had meant it. But her resolve to fight this attraction she felt for him was strengthened by this whole incident, not weakened. More than ever she felt the need to deal with him on a business level alone. She was sure her decision not to become involved with Ian was a solid one.

"You're awfully quiet."

Ian had come to stand behind her; his soft voice was close to her ear.

"What are you thinking?" he asked, placing a hand on her shoulder.

She whirled around and glared.

"Look, Ian, I've already told you that I'm not interested in any kind of relationship with you!"

"Okay!" He removed his hand and made a signal of retreat. Turning his back on her, he muttered, "Although I think you're fooling yourself."

"What?" Andrea demanded. "What was that you said?"

He faced her again, unable to hide the devilish gleam in his eye. "Damn, but it's easy to rile you. You shouldn't be such an easy target."

"Ian," she warned, "I mean it."

"I know you believe everything you're saying, okay? Now, can we drop the whole issue?"

"Yes, I think that's the best thing for us to do." Andrea flushed, sure that she'd agreed too quickly.

They stood staring at each other, Andrea uncomfortable, Ian looking cool and composed. She was searching for something to say when one of his earlier comments came to mind.

"Did you say that you ran today?" she asked.

"Umm-hmm."

A sudden excitement lit her face with a smile.
"That's great." She placed one hand on his arm. "I
missed you today."

"Oh?" That twinkle returned to his eyes.

"I *meant*," she stressed sternly, dropping her hand
to her side, "that I kept thinking you were probably
sleeping in. Letting your muscles shrivel."

"Not me," Ian assured her. "The painful memory
of getting them stretched out is still too clear."

"Good!"

They lapsed into silence once more, and Andrea was
amazed at how sensuality seemed to radiate from him.
She started to feel jumpy inside and longed for him to
say something. He appeared to be happy with the
quiet.

"W-well," she stammered. "We'll meet the same
time tomorrow?"

Ian nodded. "Take up right where we left off."

He started to leave, then turned back. "I almost
forgot. I'm supposed to invite you to dinner."

"Oh, but—"

"Denise mentioned something about a painting you
wanted to see."

"Yes," Andrea said almost to herself, remembering the special painting Denise had told her about.

"Great!"

"Oh, no, that's not what I meant."

Andrea saw his face fall and she felt a little guilty at
having misled him, no matter how unintentional it
was. "I'm a mess. I'm not dressed to go out." She
searched for an excuse.

"You are a mess," he said.

He stepped toward her. Pulling out his handkerchief, he gently rubbed a spot on her temple.

He was so close. It was as if there was no air in the room. Andrea couldn't take a breath. *Oh, God,* she thought. Why did her body react so strongly to him?

"You must have been working in the garden," he said. "I've been looking at this smudge of dirt since I arrived."

The row of cabinets behind her kept her from stepping away from him.

Do something! her mind screamed.

She snatched the hanky from his hand and rubbed at her face. "Well, why didn't you tell me?" she snapped.

"Because you look good dirty."

He laughed at her scowl.

"Denise'll be upset if I don't bring you home. She wants you to see her studio. You look fine as you are," he said. "We're only going to cook burgers on the grill."

She hated the thought of Denise being disappointed. What could it hurt? she asked herself. They wouldn't be alone with Denise and Harry there. And maybe she'd get a chance to talk to Harry again about volunteering some of his time to her track team.

"Well, let me at least wash my face." She turned and left the room.

The aroma of hamburgers grilling over hot coals was mouth watering. Stepping out onto the cedar deck, carrying an assortment of condiments to the table, Andrea looked over at Ian and smiled once again at the silly apron he was wearing—Chief Cook And

Bottle Washer, indeed. He was busy turning the meat with a long-handled utensil.

She'd had dinner at the homes of her students only twice before, and both times she and the family she'd eaten with had felt awkward, out of place. But sharing this picnic with Ian, Denise and Harry felt like the most natural thing in the world.

"Help!"

Andrea's eyes darted to where Denise was coming through the door with an armload of food and other picnic trappings: a bowl of potato salad, one of coleslaw, paper plates, napkins and plastic utensils, all precariously balanced.

"Here," Andrea offered. But as she reached for the two bowls, Denise tipped one and Andrea had to shift quickly to keep it from falling to the floor. In the process, some of the slaw dressing sloshed onto her blouse.

"Oh, I'm sorry," Denise said.

"It's okay," Andrea insisted. After setting down the food, she swiped at the spot with a napkin. "See, it's fine."

"Denise, take Andrea upstairs and help her get cleaned up," Ian suggested. Then he pointed to the grill with the turner. "It'll be a while before these are ready."

"But—" Andrea started to protest, but was interrupted by Denise's whisper.

"I can show you my painting."

They smiled at each other conspiratorially and Andrea nodded. They went inside and ran up the staircase.

Denise showed Andrea to the bathroom, and Andrea ran cold water over her soiled hem until no trace of the stain remained. She blotted it dry with a towel and smiled at Denise. "Good as new," she pronounced.

"My studio's down here."

Denise led her to the end of the hall and opened the door to a bright, sparsely furnished room. "This is it," Denise announced proudly.

"Denise, it's perfect." Andrea looked around. "It's so bright."

Windows on two sides of the room let the sun stream in most of the day. There were clean canvases leaning one against the other along the walls on one side of the room. Partially and fully completed works lined the other side.

There were two easels, one by each window, and two stools, the only furniture in the room besides a set of floor-to-ceiling wooden shelves that were crammed full of paintbrushes, tubes of pigment, turpentine and every other imaginable painter's paraphernalia.

"It's wonderful." Andrea stepped farther into the room, glancing at the paintings that lined the floor. "It looks like you've been busy."

"Oh, I haven't done all these since Dad set up the studio," Denise explained. "Most of them were stored in the back of my closet." She grinned. "Now there's plenty of room for my shoes."

Andrea studied one still life that looked so real she wanted to reach out and touch it. Another painting of a lake at sunrise captured a serene mood as a dragonfly rested on a bent reed.

"Your work is excellent."

"Thanks, but I'm frustrated that the shading on this one isn't exactly right." Denise stooped over to give the canvas a critical examination.

Andrea moved to stand beside her.

"Well, it looks good to me, but then I don't know a whole lot about art."

"See—" Denise crouched down "—the light was..." Her voice faded and she stood and smiled. "You don't need to hear me complain."

"Maybe Mr. Webster can help." Andrea mentioned the school's art instructor before remembering the rumor that he wasn't a very talented painter.

She could tell by Denise's reaction or lack of reaction rather, that the teenager wasn't thrilled with the suggestion.

"This is the painting I'm doing for Pops." Denise uncovered one of the easels to display an unfinished depiction of a small trophy sitting on a table. A cleated running shoe lying on its side was penciled in, waiting to be painted. Bright ribbons and medals looked as though they'd been tossed around the base of the tall golden trophy.

"It's wonderful," Andrea said.

"That's what Pops won at the first Wilmington Challenge."

"He'll love it!"

"I hope so. I'm going to try to have it finished so I can give it to him the day of the race."

"It's going to be a day he'll never forget."

While Denise covered the painting, Andrea went back over to the still life she'd admired earlier. The colors of the flowers lying beside a vase intrigued her.

Pale mauves, pinks and blues mingled with several different shades of green.

"I like this," she said finally.

"It's my favorite, too." Denise stuffed her hands into the pockets of her shorts. "I've been thinking of going into town to see if one of the shop owners would take it on consignment."

"Denise, that's a great idea!"

Andrea was proud that Denise had the wherewithal to make plans to utilize her talent.

Denise shrugged self-consciously. "Maybe I could pay Dad back for all the supplies he's bought me lately."

Draping her arm around the teenager's shoulders, Andrea said, "From what your dad tells me, you two have been spending a lot of time together."

Light danced in Denise's eyes. "Yes, and it's been so great. I'm glad you're training him for the half marathon. He's home more often, and I've never had this much time with him before."

"I'm glad," Andrea said.

"You know..." Denise's smile vanished and she looked at Andrea solemnly. "He couldn't help missing the meet."

The girl's tone told Andrea that Denise felt the need to defend her father.

"I understand that." Andrea nodded.

"He called to explain why he had to stay over. I shouldn't have been so disappointed."

Denise's eyes pleaded for Andrea's approval.

"Your dad explained everything to me, too," Andrea assured the girl. "You're right, he had no other choice but to stay."

Denise smiled timidly, relief filling her eyes.

"Come and get it!" Harry's voice filtered up to them, and they started for the door.

"You go ahead," Andrea said, stopping at the bathroom. "I want to powder my nose."

She slipped into the room and shut the door. Taking a deep breath, she stared at her image in the mirror as a wave of memories flooded through her.

Denise's excuses for Ian concerned her. She remembered experiencing the same powerful ache to justify her own father's behavior many years ago. When she was young, she'd invented the dream that he'd had no other choice but to take care of his business interests.

It hadn't been until she'd grown up that she'd let herself believe the truth: he'd loved his business more than he'd loved his own daughter, and he had been the only kind of father he could be. A lousy one.

After realizing the truth about Robert, Andrea had stopped making excuses for him and had started blaming him instead. And it had done her a world of good.

She leaned back against the door, wondering how long it would take Denise to stop absolving Ian and start reproaching him.

Sure, Ian had been home for the last month, and Denise had been in heaven, but after the half marathon, he would probably go straight back to his previous routine. Then how long would it take Denise to wake up and see what kind of relationship she really had with her father? How long before her blinded love for him turned to accusing scorn as Andrea's had for Robert?

Andrea sighed despondently, hating the thought of how such a revelation might embitter Denise and wishing there was something she could do about it.

"Those hamburgers were delicious," Andrea complimented, wiping her fingers with a napkin.

"Thank you." Ian reclined in his seat.

Harry rubbed his stomach, saying, "I'm filled to the brim."

"Help me clean up, Pops?" Denise asked Harry as she started gathering the paper plates into a pile.

"Oh, I'll help with that," Andrea offered quickly, hopping up from her seat.

"I'm no invalid." Harry practically growled the words, and Andrea froze.

"I didn't... I'm sorry." Andrea swallowed and lowered herself back into her chair.

Harry snatched the bowl that held what little remained of the potato salad and set it in his lap before wheeling his chair toward the door. The edge of his wheelchair caught an aluminum lounger that was sitting on the deck and he dragged it several inches. He stopped and thrust the chair away from him and it clattered loudly.

"I didn't mean to hurt his feelings," Andrea said to Ian after the his father had entered the house.

"I know you didn't." Ian reached over and squeezed her hand reassuringly. "He's been awfully sensitive since I arrived this morning. Something must have happened while I was away, but I have no idea what it could have been."

His skin felt warm against her fingers, and his thumb began to make tiny circles across her knuckles. Her heart fluttered and she pulled her fingers from his grasp and placed her hands in her lap.

"So," she said, hoping he didn't observe the anxiety that was churning inside her, "I'm glad you increased your mileage today."

"You know, it wasn't as tough this time."

He gave her an easy smile, and Andrea was almost sure he hadn't noticed her reaction to his touch.

"Good." Andrea leaned toward the table. "Ian, I've been wanting to ask you something..When I saw you in the restaurant and snuffed out your cigarette in your drink—" she blushed as she brought up the incident "—I told you that you should consider quitting. I haven't seen you with a cigarette since. Have you had any trouble?"

Ian laughed. "You *demanded* that I stop."

"Yes, well..." Andrea's color deepened, and Ian laughed harder.

"No," he said. "I didn't have any trouble quitting because I never indulged in the habit to begin with."

"But—"

"It was Pamela's cigarette." Ian's eyes lit with humor as Andrea's face turned beet red.

Andrea groaned, covering her eyes with her hand. "I'm so embarrassed."

"She didn't mind," he told her. "As a matter of fact, she thought it was funny. She was delighted. Her exact words were, 'There's one lady who just might be able to handle you.'"

He rested his chin on his fist and stared at her a moment before softly saying, "And, you know, I think she may be right."

His eyes took on a warm glow and Andrea's breath caught in her throat.

"Well, I—I," Andrea stammered, "I *am* a tough coach."

Her eyes darted from her hands that were folded on the table in front of her to his face and back again. She was sure he was about to say something else, but Denise came outside and plopped down in her seat.

"You guys look guilty as sin," she observed, laughing. "What've ya been doin'? Making plans to rob a bank or something?"

"I was just telling Andrea about Pamela."

"Oh, Pamela!" Denise exclaimed, her face lighting up. "She's wonderful! She works for Dad. And she's been doing all his traveling so he can be at home."

"But not without a hefty raise, I might add," Ian said.

Denise turned adoring eyes on her father. "But it's been worth it."

"It's been worth it." He nodded, giving his daughter a warm smile, and then gazed at Andrea.

"But what about her family?" Andrea asked. "Won't they be upset with her traveling so much?"

"No way," Denise said. "She's been harping on Dad to promote her for ages."

"Denise is right," Ian agreed. "Pam's a real career woman. And she loves to travel."

Harry joined them then; all traces of his earlier ill humor were gone.

"Tell your dad about the relay race yesterday," he said to Denise.

"Well, Miss O'Connor had all of us practice passing the baton all week, so we were ready." Denise's shoulders leveled proudly. "She had me running the first leg of the race. I'm not quick, but I have staying power. Right?" Denise directed her question at Andrea.

"You bet," Andrea agreed.

"Are you kidding me?" Harry commented. "You flew around that track."

"I was scared to death that the other runners would pass me." Denise laughed.

Harry looked at them all, his face animated. "And I've never seen a smoother baton handoff. All those kids did a great job yesterday." He eyed Andrea. "You're a good coach."

"Hear, hear!" Ian added, lifting his can of soda to his lips.

"Thanks," Andrea murmured.

"And that girl who won the high jump..." Harry snapped his fingers in the air, trying to recall the name.

"Sara." Denise and Andrea offered it in unison.

"That's the one." Harry's craggy face took on a youthful glow. "That's a rare technique she uses, lifting her pelvis at the height of her jump. I don't know how she does it."

"You know, I've studied her jumping style every day and I can't figure it out, either." Andrea grinned. "Sara doesn't even realize she's doing it."

"If you could figure out how she maneuvers her body that way," Harry said, resting his elbows on the arms of his chair, "you could get the other jumpers to try it, too."

Andrea inhaled deeply, brushing her fingers through her hair as an idea hit her.

"Would you consider coming to track practice this week, so we can watch Sara together? Maybe between the two of us, we can figure out what she's doing."

A strained hush fell over the table, and Andrea had an instant to regret her request. She could see Denise out of the corner of her eye, sitting frozen, waiting. Andrea wondered what Ian must be thinking.

Harry wore a closed expression. But slowly color filled his face, and Andrea could see his anger quickly building.

She suddenly wished she hadn't said anything and wondered what she could say to make things right.

"I'll understand if . . ." she began.

Harry's open palm crashing down on the table top silenced her.

"When will people learn that I don't want or *need* their pity!"

Without waiting for a reply, he wheeled himself inside.

Chapter Seven

"Pops!" Denise fled from the table and disappeared into the house.

Andrea stared at the empty doorway, horror stricken that she'd offended Harry. She hadn't meant to intrude, but she'd been so sure he could really help her students.

When Ian's warm hand enveloped hers, she turned toward him.

"I'm sorry about this," he said. "I'm going to go talk to him. I'll only be a minute."

Ian rose, but Andrea clasped his hand in both of her own.

"Wait," she pleaded. "I think I know what's wrong."

Ian lowered himself back into his chair, an inquiring look in his eyes.

Holding on to Ian's hand comforted her and made the telling easier.

"It all started yesterday," she explained. "During the track meet, I asked Harry if he'd consider coming to practice to coach the kids." She searched Ian's face for signs of disapproval, but saw none. "He knows so much about running. He shouldn't let all his knowledge go to waste."

She hoped Ian understood her motives. Her reasons for asking Harry hadn't been selfish. Sure, her runners would benefit from Harry's influence, but she was sure Harry would gain from the experience, too.

Andrea knew there was no way she could give Harry the ability to run, but if she could get him involved in the sport again, even in a small way, she could help him to see that his life was far from over.

She probed Ian's expression. Did he understand?

His features were somber, pensive.

"I must be blind," he finally said.

Andrea's brow knit with confusion, and Ian sighed heavily before explaining.

"The first time I met you, you told me that my relationship with my daughter wasn't all it could be. And you were right." He looked away a moment, as though gathering the courage to speak. "And now you're telling me that my father isn't happy."

His eyes returned to hers, his gaze fervent and heavy.

"And again I see that you're correct in your observation. My father isn't content with his life, I see that now. But how is it that I've lived in the same house with Denise and my father and I haven't recognized their needs?"

Andrea's heart twisted at the look of self-reproach on Ian's face. From the very first, she'd wanted to make him see his shortcomings as a father. But she was sure that it had had more to do with her relationship with Robert, her own father, rather than Ian's relationship with Denise. Somehow she'd thought that pointing out Ian's fatherly flaws would purge herself of her own agonizing memories. But she was wrong.

She was filled with misery at the thought of having induced Ian to feel guilty. What had she been thinking? Had she meant to hurt him?

Weeks ago, she would have answered yes to that question. But she knew him now. She knew that he loved Denise, that he'd never meant to harm or disappoint his daughter. And Harry's plight had nothing whatsoever to do with Ian. Andrea felt compelled to tell him so.

Releasing his hand only long enough to slide her chair closer to him, she once again entwined her fingers with his. "Ian, Harry's problem is just that—Harry's." She rushed to clarify her statement as a frown creased Ian's forehead. "What I mean is, it's wonderful that you want to help your father. But until he wants our help, no one can do a blessed thing."

Ian's expression was closed. Andrea wished she knew what he was thinking.

Finally, he slipped his hand from her grasp.

"You're probably right," he said, rising. "But I should still go talk to him."

"Ian."

He stopped and looked down at her.

"I'm the one who upset him in the first place," she said. "He thinks I feel sorry for him. The best person to tell him I don't—" she pushed her chair back from the table "—is me." She lifted her gaze to Ian's. "Do you mind if I talk to him first?" she asked.

Ian silently nodded, and Andrea went into the house.

Following Denise's voice, she found the teenager standing in the hallway on the first floor, pleading with her grandfather through a closed door.

When Denise saw Andrea approaching, she met her halfway down the hall.

"I've never seen him so shook up," Denise said. "I can't get him to let me in."

"Well—" Andrea gave Denise's shoulder a gentle squeeze "—would you go outside with your dad and let me give it a try?"

"Sure," Denise said, nodding.

Andrea waited until Denise had turned the corner before she knocked on Harry's door.

"Harry, it's Andrea," she called. "I'd like to talk to you."

Pressing her ear against the door, all she heard was silence.

She knocked again. "I won't go away, Harry. And I'm just as stubborn as you are, so you might as well open up."

His mumbling could be heard as he turned the lock on the door and let it swing open.

"Can't a man have any privacy?" he grumbled, as he turned his wheelchair back around, gliding toward the center of the room.

His back was to her as she entered, and she took the time to let her eyes rove around the room.

Her breath caught at the sight of all the framed awards and ribbons that were hung on the walls. Two large wooden shelves were filled to overflowing with trophies, small silver and pewter plates and ceramic mugs, all engraved with Harry's name.

When Harry faced her, he offered her the trophy that had been resting in his lap.

"I won this at the first Wilmington Challenge," he said. "It's the trophy I'm proudest of winning."

She cradled the trophy, a miniature runner bolted to a wooden base, the very one Denise had depicted in her painting. Andrea looked it up and down, her mind racing with what she should say, how she should apologize.

"Harry," she began, "I'm sorry about what happened out there."

Harry made an indignant "humph," his shoulders jerking upward. "I've gotten used to it."

A spark of anger leapt inside her. Harry was so cocksure of her motives.

"Used to what?" she challenged.

"The sympathy I see on people's faces. The pity in their words."

"Harry," Andrea said dryly, "you didn't ever see sympathy in *my* face or hear pity in *my* voice."

His eyes narrowed and he opened his mouth to speak, but Andrea dared him to dispute with a lift of her eyebrows.

As her gaze dipped to Harry's lifeless legs and then lifted again to take in the frustration defined on his face, she wondered how deep-rooted his problem really was and why he hadn't sought help before.

Her quipping remark seemed to relax him, and she continued. "Look at all this," she said, sweeping out her arm in a grand gesture to indicate the room full of awards. "Who in his right mind could feel sympathy for a man who's had such a wonderful life up to this point?" She tucked the small trophy in both hands as though she were holding a precious relic.

"You asked me to help coach the track team," he accused.

"I did," she agreed with a nod. "Harry, you have more knowledge of the sport in your little finger than most people could learn in a lifetime."

He looked away, flushing almost sheepishly. "But I thought you were feeling sorry for a crippled old man."

"Harry," Andrea said, her tone somber as she eased herself down on the edge of the bed, "just because you're handicapped doesn't mean people are feeling sorry for you." She tilted her head. "Granted, some will. But I think the majority of people today have learned that a physical disability doesn't diminish a person's mental capabilities." Looking him square in the eyes, she asked, "Why haven't you ever talked about your feelings with anyone?"

He looked astounded, as though her question was a bolt from the blue. "But—" He shook his head. "Who?"

"How about Ian?" she suggested. "Your son loves you very much, you know."

"Ian works sixteen hour days most of the time." He frowned. "He's too busy building up his business to be burdened with my problems."

Andrea just looked at him. "How do you think Ian would feel about what you've just said?" she asked. "He cares about you, and you know he'd be upset to hear how you feel."

Harry averted his gaze.

"Even if you didn't want to talk to Ian, the phone book must list pages and pages of counselors trained to help."

"There's nothing wrong with me," he insisted. "Nothing that being a contributing member of society wouldn't cure." His chin lifted a fraction. "I need to feel useful."

"Useful?" Her incredulity burst forth like a sprinter out of the starting blocks. "From what I've heard, you've helped raise Ian's daughter for quite some time now. You've taken care of the brunt of his family concerns and his home while he's been making a name for himself. Wouldn't you call that being useful?"

Harry shrugged and nodded vaguely.

"Besides," she said wryly, "I'm giving you a chance to be useful with my request for your help."

Harry shook his head. "I'd like to, but I just couldn't do it."

"Sure, you could."

"I couldn't do it!" His lips thinned with determination.

"Why not?" Andrea knew she was pushing, but she needed to know.

"You saw what happened to that girl out there on the track yesterday, the hurdler who fell." Harry planted his fist on the arm of his chair. "What if I'd been coaching her? What could I have done?"

"You would have done exactly as I did," Andrea said, "dusted off her pride and sent her to finish the race."

Harry studied her face. "You make it sound so easy."

"And it would be," she stated emphatically.

He shook his head.

"Harry, you wouldn't ever be alone," she argued. "I'll be there, the kids will be there."

Again he shook his head, unmoved.

Now she knew from whom Ian inherited his bullheadedness. She thought a moment and decided to use another tack.

"Harry, you have Ian training to run for a half marathon. It's not something he would have ever attempted on his own. He's not doing it for himself, he's doing this for you. Because he loves you."

She looked at the old man, whose eyes were now downcast.

"And Denise. I'm sure she'd love to spend all her time painting, but she's training because it makes you happy. Because she, too, loves you very much."

Setting the trophy on the dresser by the door, Andrea took a deep breath, gathering the courage to say what she knew needed to be said.

"Your family is giving you a lot, Harry. Don't you think it's time you gave a little?"

He inhaled sharply at her question but stayed silent. His face was unreadable. Andrea couldn't tell if he was feeling hurt or angry. She hadn't meant to hurt him, she only wanted to make him think. Andrea hoped her little nudge would push him far enough to make a decision, a decision that might change the rest of his life.

His expression remained masked, and Andrea realized that she'd done all she could. The next step was up to him. She stood up and left him to weigh her words.

"Thanks for dinner, Ian. I had a great time."

As soon as Ian's car slowed to a stop at the curb in front of her house, Andrea opened the door and stepped out.

"Wait a second," Ian called, turning off the car's engine and getting out himself.

The spring air had turned chilly, and the sky was overcast. The moon glowed eerily through smoky clouds. Andrea crossed her arms and hugged herself as she waited for him.

"I wanted to talk to you," he said, grasping her arm and pulling her up the walkway.

"If it's about Harry, I told you, I apologized."

"It's not about Harry," he said.

"It's your schedule, isn't it?" She eyed him critically. "You're not going to complain that it's too hard again?"

"No, no." He waved his hand in the air. "It's not that, either."

She stopped on the front step. "Then what?"

"Let's get inside," he suggested. "You need a sweater."

Andrea turned the key in the lock and was greeted by Gunther's welcoming barks. She flipped on a couple of lights and picked up a sweatshirt that was lying on a chair in the living room.

Pushing her arms and head into the shirt, she asked, "So, what's up?"

"Well..." Ian sat on the couch and began rubbing the knuckles of one hand into the palm of the other.

"This must be personal," she said, sitting in the chair opposite him. "Is it Denise?"

"No!"

"Well, what, then?"

"It's us," he blurted out. "I want you to have dinner with me."

Andrea's eyes narrowed. "Ian, I've told you—"

"I know what you've told me and I know your reasons. Just hear me out for a minute." He stood and paced the room.

Andrea was alert and wary as she watched him parade back and forth in front of her. She'd done everything in her power to avoid a personal relationship with Ian up to this point. She'd completely suppressed her physical reactions to him. She'd spelled out exactly how she felt about their becoming involved. Why, then, was he pursuing the matter?

He stopped directly in front of her and stared down at her a long moment.

"I know you've said that I'm not the kind of man you want to become involved with. And I have to agree that when I first met you, I had some problems with Denise." He stuffed his hands deep into his pockets. "But I've taken steps to change that. I'd hoped that you would see that."

"And I have," Andrea assured him softly, but she kept her tone unemotional.

"But it hasn't changed your mind about me?"

"Ian…" Her voice trailed off. Wanting to keep the promise she'd made to herself about becoming involved with Ian, she refused to admit to the desire she felt for him.

An intense silence stood between them.

"You do something to me, Andrea," was all he said.

Finally Andrea gave in to the nervous laughter that gathered in her throat, and she said, "That's a good line, Ian."

"Andrea." Anger flashed in his eyes and he dragged her to her feet.

His touch was like a jolt of electricity, a living current that paralyzed her.

"I don't believe you're as cool as you pretend to be." His eyes raked her features up and down with excruciating slowness. "I see your body's reaction to me and it's just as strong as mine is to you."

Andrea drew her gaze away from him, and mumbled, "I don't know what you're talking about."

"You're a liar!"

She twisted out of his grasp and glared at him.

"Look, Ian. I never led you to believe that there would ever be any more to this than a straight business deal." She flung the words at him. "You knew from the first that I wanted something from you and you wanted something from me. Straight and simple."

Ian inhaled deeply and the anger seemed to drain from him as he expelled the breath. He rubbed his hand back and forth across his jaw, then let his hand drop to his side as he asked, "Could it be that what we wanted from each other has changed?" He gently placed his fingers against her lips. "Don't answer that now," he said. "Just think about it."

When he was gone, she lowered herself into the chair, rested her head against its cushion and stared off into space.

Andrea entered the school auditorium and took a seat in the last row, near the door. The room was filling with parents, students, teachers and administrators. This was the last home-school meeting of the year, and tonight's topic was the budget.

"Good evening, Miss O'Connor." Ian slid past her and sat down in the seat next to her.

Andrea couldn't suppress the smile that his formal greeting brought to her lips. It had been three days since he had tried to barricade her into an emotional corner. Their daily runs had gone on as usual, their stretching routine lasting longer each day as their conversations became more prolonged. But even though she had refused to comment on his asking her out, he continued to be excessively gallant and charming. She knew his winsome behavior was his way of getting close to her, of getting her to see he was harmless.

But he wasn't harmless. Her reaction to him wasn't harmless. She instinctively knew that if she wanted to stay safe, she needed to steer clear of any personal involvement with Ian.

"I've never been to one of these meetings," Ian admitted. "What's going to be discussed?"

"Next year's budget, mostly," she said.

When Andrea saw Mr. Scott approach the microphone, she leaned toward Ian and whispered, "I'm hoping to get more—" Just then, the school's principal tapped on the mike and started his opening address.

"Good evening," he said. "I want to welcome you to Highland and thank you for coming tonight. I want to get right down to business and talk about the main reason that all of you are here—money." He gave a little chuckle. "I'm sure all of you are wondering how the school board has decided to spend your hard-earned dollars. I'd like for everyone to look at this handout." He stepped from behind the lectern and passed a stack of papers to the people in the front row. "So, if you'll please take one and pass the rest toward the back, we can get started."

Mr. Scott shuffled his notes on the lectern and cleared his throat. "As you can see, there have been a few changes in the proposed budget, the biggest of which is the monies that had been allocated to the physical education department will now be spent on computer software and relandscaping of the school grounds."

Andrea couldn't hold in her astonished gasp.

"Miss O'Connor, would you please stand," Mr. Scott requested.

Heads turned in her direction, and Andrea slowly rose to her feet, forcing a plastic smile on her lips.

"I'd like to thank Miss O'Connor," Mr. Scott said, more to the crowd than to her, "and let all of you know how she's undertaken the task of volunteering her time in exchange for a donation that will enable the physical-education department to purchase equipment that had previously been among our projected expenditures."

Andrea quickly sat down after enduring a sparse applause. Cold fury directed at Mr. Scott froze in the pit of her stomach as the same question reverberated in her brain over and over. How could he take her money away? How?

She was absolutely livid. She stared unseeingly at the paper that had been thrust at her by the man sitting in front of her. Not only was she angry, she felt betrayed.

Mr. Scott and the rest of the school-board members knew that Ian's donation wasn't going to be enough to cover the cost of all the equipment that was needed. Her anger slowly evolved into a dark disappointment that clouded her mind.

But when she focused on the numbers that were printed on the report in her hand, her anger burned anew. She had to get out of that room before she did something rash, something that might get her into a lot of trouble.

Crumpling the paper in her fist, she snatched up her purse and sweater and left the auditorium.

She marched down the empty corridor, shoved open the heavy doors and went out into the night.

The chilly May air filled her lungs, and she walked out onto the side yard of the school, then farther onto the track. Tossing her soft angora sweater across her shoulders, she stared out at the track and wished she'd had appropriate running clothes and shoes so she could work off her frustration.

"Andrea!"

Startled, she turned to see Ian coming down the mound of grass toward her.

"You looked upset," he said, reaching out for her. "Like you might need someone to talk to."

The warmth of his hands on her shoulders penetrated the softness of her sweater and the silky material of her blouse, and she was instantly consumed by a sea of calm. She closed her eyes and let the feeling of solid security his presence generated wash over her.

When she raised her eyelids, she was astonished to see that his image was blurred by her tears and she quickly turned away, embarrassed. But he didn't relinquish his hold.

"Hey," he said softly, pressing against her shoulders, "talk to me."

"It's stupid," she said, dashing away the tears.

He pulled out his handkerchief and offered it to her. She took it and twisted it in her fingers.

"It's the money," she admitted. "Mr. Scott knew that what you planned to give the school was only a portion of what I needed."

"I see." He took the linen hanky from her and gently swiped it across her damp eyelashes.

"I feel like such a baby." Andrea sniffed and tried to smile. "But you can't imagine how important this was to me."

"I think I can," he said. "You're coaching me, and I know it's the *last* thing you wanted to do."

"That was before I knew you could do it."

He raised an eyebrow. "You think I can do it now?"

She nodded. "I know you can. You've worked hard. I don't mind helping someone who wants to be helped."

He took her hand, and they walked to the center of the football field.

"About the money," he said. "Maybe you can talk to the board again."

"I'll try—" she shook her head "—but the chances are slim to none. I'll just have to make do with your donation."

"Who knows," he said. "Maybe something will come up."

His supportive words lightened her heart. It didn't matter that he said them only because he was trying to cheer her, in fact, that made them mean even more.

She looked up at the clear night sky; the stars glittered like diamonds against black velvet. Holding Ian's hand gave her comfort; it felt natural. She knew she should let go, but all she wanted at this moment was the solace his touch provided.

She sighed. "Thanks, Ian."

"I didn't do anything," he said, his voice caressing her ears.

"You did a lot." She turned to face him. "How have you put up with me all these weeks?"

"I'll admit, it's been tough." The grin on his face told her he was teasing.

They came upon a soccer ball in the middle of the field, and Ian let go of her hand and dribbled the ball several feet.

"Think you can take it away from me?" he called over his shoulder.

She laughed at his antics.

"I mean it," he said. "Think you can?"

Her eyebrows rose at the challenge. "I know I can." She kicked off her heels and trotted after him.

He maneuvered the ball around her and deftly kept it just out of her reach.

"Very impressive moves, Mr. Powers!"

He stopped and grinned at her. "I know."

She took advantage of the moment and stole the ball, dribbling it in the opposite direction.

"Hey!" he called, running after her.

He bent over and snatched the ball up in his hands and laughed as he abruptly changed direction again.

Her jaw jutted with determination and she raced three paces before springing onto his back.

Ian's pace slowed, but he stubbornly trudged ahead.

"What is this, a new strategy?" he groaned.

She laughed in his ear. "You changed this into a free-for-all when you picked up the ball."

His steps became heavy, and his exaggerated theatrics of staggering under her weight made her laugh even harder. Finally, he fell to his knees and they tumbled to the ground. Ian let the ball slip from his grasp and turned to face her, staring, unsmiling, into her eyes.

"It's beautiful out here," Ian said, encircling her in his arms.

She nodded, splaying her hands, one atop the other, on his chest.

The night was utterly quiet; the moon cast shadows on his face. It was such a handsome face, she thought. His dark eyes were as soft as the velvet sky.

She realized at that moment that she liked Ian Powers. She never meant to, but she did. And he made her feel... She inhaled deeply and looked down at him. He made her feel so good. She grinned.

"I took the ball," she said.

"Not without cheating." He raised his knee and shifted a fraction.

"I didn't cheat," she said with mock indignation. "Didn't anyone ever tell you that you must take every advantage?"

"Take every advantage, huh?" His voice was like silk, smooth and rich.

She fought, but she was helpless against the slow smile that spread across her lips. "Don't tell me you're planning to take advantage of me?"

"Oh, no." He lifted his hands from where they'd been resting on her back, opening them wide. "I took advantage of the last time we were in this position." He looked around him. "Well, almost this position."

Her smile widened. "What are you suggesting, Mr. Powers?" Her teasing words were sultry, and she marveled at the luxurious sensuality that seemed to envelope them like a warm blanket.

His eyes darkened with the heat of passion until they were as black as the night.

"I'm suggesting, Miss O'Connor," he whispered, "that you heed your own advice."

Chapter Eight

Her smile disappeared without a trace. An intense desire was etched in the set of his jaw, his eyes were ablaze with fiery light. She knew what he wanted her to do. And she didn't intend to disappoint him.

Promises be damned! she thought. She wanted this, right here, right now. This moment was all that mattered.

She moved with excruciating slowness, lower and lower, until her lips met his.

Her kiss was at first tentative, timid, and he let her explore. But as a liquid fire began to pulse through her veins, she was no longer satisfied with just the feel of his lips. She needed to touch him, to savor him. And she did.

Her tongue parted his lips and she tasted him with hungry boldness. His mouth was warm and faintly sweet.

She slid one hand around his neck, his hair brushing against the sensitive skin of her wrist. Her other hand traveled over the bunched muscles of his shoulder, and she pushed his arm back around her, needing to feel his embrace.

Her breasts pressed into his broad chest and a shiver rippled down her spine. She wanted more, needed more.

When he tensed the muscles of his arms to crush her to him and raged war on her mouth with his tongue, she welcomed it, reveled in it.

Her breathing was ragged when she lifted her head a fraction, softly rubbing her lips back and forth against his, relishing the feel and smell of him.

He opened his eyes and stared at her.

"That was nice," he whispered.

"But, I'm not finished yet." She gave him a lecherous grin.

He took a deep breath, sliding his hands over her back.

"I'd hoped not," he said, chuckling deep in the back of his throat. He brought one hand to cradle the back of her head and pulled her to him.

When his mouth covered hers, it was as though the earth rumbled and rolled. The blood pounded in her ears and she was sure the clear night sky must be full of booming thunder. She expected to be drenched any minute by the storm that had so quickly moved over them.

But when Ian broke the kiss and nuzzled his face against her neck, she opened her eyes and lifted her head to see the stars sparkling in the moonlit darkness and was once again amazed by her body's reaction to this man.

She lowered her head and smoothed her cheek against his clean-shaven skin. His cologne was rich and spicy and she breathed it deeply. She exhaled and felt his fingers running through her hair. She turned her head toward his touch and his fingers stroked her cheekbone and along her jaw.

Ian shifted and brought her beneath him. He outlined her eyebrows with his fingertip and then lightly rubbed the lobe of her ear.

When he said, "I didn't think you'd do it," she only smiled at him.

"Listen, Andrea," he said, his expression intensifying, "I want to spend some time with you. Besides the training, I mean. I want to take you out."

"Okay." Her voice was barely audible.

"I mean it!" He apparently didn't hear her, his brow wrinkling with feeling. "I want to take you to dinner."

"Ian, I said okay."

His expression relaxed into a warm smile and she laughed softly.

"Okay," he repeated.

He leaned over and kissed her tenderly on the mouth, then lifted his head to look at her. When she felt his touch, she lowered her eyelids. His finger, feather light, traced a line down the bridge of her nose, over its small, rounded tip, across the bow of her lips, down to her chin. His touch drew lower, along her neck to the hollow of her throat. He paused there to lightly kiss the delicate depression.

Andrea's breathing quickened with the brush of his warm breath on the tender skin of her neck. Pushing her sweater from her shoulders, he deftly unbuttoned her silk blouse, and his kisses lowered with each button that was freed.

She raised her hand and buried it in his thick hair. This is crazy, she thought. What if someone saw them? But even the risk of being seen didn't put out the fire of her desire. She didn't want this to end. Not now. Not ever.

The silky material whispered across her skin as he laid aside the facing of her blouse, his warm hand sliding over her stomach and ribs. When his thumb grazed the underside of her breast, her breath caught and held.

His eyes searched hers for…what? She didn't know. What she did know was that she wanted to feel his lips on hers once more.

"Kiss me," she pleaded.

He groaned and pressed his mouth to hers. His hand slid over the lacy material of her bra to caress her rounded breast, his thumb finding the aroused bud of her nipple.

Absolute paradise, she thought. It would be so easy to lose herself all together.

Dragging her mouth from his, she moaned his name.

"I know," he said. "This has to stop."

His gaze held hers an instant longer as he rubbed his thumb over her swollen lips. Then she watched him lean up and carefully button her blouse. She noticed that he was breathing deeply and evenly the entire time he straightened her clothing. Finally, he gently tugged her sweater back onto her shoulders. Andrea didn't rush him. She, too, needed all the time she could get to compose herself.

It awed her, the way they were together; like a spark meeting dry tinder; like thunder and lightning.

Ian stood, smoothing his hands down along his pants legs, and Andrea sat up. She grasped his outstretched hand and he hoisted her up. With his arm encircling her shoulders, they walked back toward the school.

"I have to go back to Connecticut tomorrow morning," Ian told her. "I'll need to spend about four days there, checking in on the factory workers and the plant. And there's something else I need to look into."

He stopped at the double doors of the school building and turned her to face him.

"Will you have dinner with me Monday night?" he asked.

She nodded. "Will you stick with your training?"

"Of course, I will," he assured her. "I'll even take my schedule along with me." His voice took on a huskiness as he added, "I'll run at the same time we usually do, so we'll still be running together."

Andrea felt suddenly shy and averted her gaze, but he gently captured her face between his hands and brought his lips to touch hers in a sweet, tender kiss.

"Until Monday," he said.

"Until Monday," she whispered back.

Those next four days were the longest of Andrea's life. She hadn't realized how much she'd come to enjoy spending her mornings with Ian. After running without him that first morning, she understood that they'd been doing more than just exercising their bodies together; they had talked and listened to each other. And now, without him, Andrea felt utterly alone.

She'd taken Gunther with her, hoping to miss Ian less, but it hadn't worked. She missed his rich laughter, his handsome face, those dark eyes.

Knowing that he was running, too, even if he was hundreds of miles away, made it a little easier. But only a little.

She sat at her desk, tapping her pencil on her attendance book as she waited for the bell that would start her day.

It was hard to have the Monday-morning blues when she was so excited at the thought of spending the evening with Ian.

She'd argued with herself all weekend about her decision to go out with him. But she'd rationalized that her promise to keep their relationship strictly business had been made before she'd really come to know him.

Ian was a caring man, a loving father. She knew that now. Sure, he'd made some mistakes, but he was only human. Who *didn't* make mistakes sometimes? The important thing was to learn from those mistakes. And Ian had. She'd been wrong to compare Ian to her own father.

Hadn't Ian been spending more time with his daughter? Hadn't he shown Andrea that he was concerned about Harry's happiness? Hadn't he proved that he was serious in his commitment to run this half marathon?

All these questions had helped to bolster her during the past four days. But a small shadow of doubt kept rearing its ugly head. What would happen after Ian ran the Wilmington Challenge? Would he shed his coat of loving father, caring son and would-be lover and slip once more into the guise of slick entrepreneur?

Andrea shoved the haunting questions aside for the thousandth time. She wanted to pursue a relationship with Ian. What would come of it, she didn't know, but she refused to let her anxiety about the future get in the way.

A light tap on her office door caught her attention and she called, "Come in."

Denise poked her head around the door.

"Hi," she said. "Could I talk to you?"

"Sure." Andrea smiled brightly at Ian's daughter. "Come on in."

Denise sat down, balancing a pile of books on her lap. "Dad's home."

A wave of giddy excitement rushed through Andrea. She did her best to tamp it down and focused on Denise's face.

A tiny frown knit the teenager's brow, and Andrea leaned toward her, tilting her head.

"Is something wrong?" she asked.

"No...yes..." Denise looked close to tears. "Oh, I don't know!" She sat back and jammed her finger into her mouth to nibble at her nail.

"What's this all about?" Andrea coaxed.

"Why would he want to send me away?" Denise's words sounded young and frightened.

"Send you away?"

Denise jostled her books and pulled out a pamphlet from among them and handed it to Andrea.

On the front cover was the name of a prominent cultural-arts boarding school located in Connecticut. Andrea's eyes narrowed with perplexity, and she turned the booklet over in her hand, not really reading it.

"I don't understand," she said, looking up at Denise. "Your dad wants you to live here?" She indicated the picture of the prestigious school. "To go to school here?"

Denise nodded slowly, her features grave.

"Okay," Andrea said, rubbing her fingers back and forth across her forehead. "Let's just take a minute and assess the situation." She opened the information pamphlet and scanned its contents.

"It looks like a good school, Denise." She read further. "A very good school."

"I know," Denise said. "Dad read it to me, and I read it, too." She heaved a sigh. "I'm just not sure I want to live so far away."

"I can understand that." Andrea glanced at Denise. "What did your father say when you told him that?"

"I didn't. I couldn't! He was so excited about it, I couldn't tell him that it was a lousy idea." She shook her head. "I'm not even sure it *is* a lousy idea."

Andrea lifted her eyebrows questioningly.

"I mean," Denise continued, "if he *wants* me to go..."

"But what you want is important, too," Andrea pointed out.

Denise's posture seemed to deflate. "This had to happen just when Dad was spending more time at home." She lifted her eyes to Andrea's. "Is it dumb of me to want to make him happy? Make him proud of me?"

"Of course, it isn't," Andrea said. "And from what this information says, you could get some wonderful art instruction."

"Well," Denise said, shrugging one shoulder, "my painting's only a hobby, anyway."

"Denise, you know it means more to you than that." Andrea's expression was gently chiding.

"But not more than being with Dad and Pops!" Denise blurted.

Andrea rested her elbow on her desk and planted her chin on her fist.

"Well, what would you like to do?" she asked. "And how can I help?"

Denise's face brightened perceptively. "Would you talk to Dad? See how set he is on my going away to school?"

Andrea's heart dipped a little. She knew that this subject would more than likely cause an argument between herself and Ian. But she stared at Denise and nodded anyway.

"Sure, I'll talk to him."

Andrea stroked powdered blush lightly on her cheeks with a small feathery brush, then looked into the mirror to study her reflection. A touch of lipstick and she'd be ready for her dinner date with Ian.

She'd teetered back and forth between excitement and apprehension so many times when thinking of tonight that her stomach was twisted in jittery knots.

The kisses they'd shared on the athletic field the night of the school meeting had provoked many a daydream. And, with her conscious mind unable to control them, her night dreams had been wildly abandoned, her and Ian's caresses becoming more and more intimate each time she closed her eyes in slumber.

The excitement over seeing him again made her giddy.

Leaning into the mirror, she smoothed rich color on her lips. She brushed her blond hair until it fell around her face in a shining cap. She set the brush on the counter and seeing the tiny frown between her eyes, she turned away from her image.

Why would Ian want to send Denise to school in Connecticut? Why did he want his daughter to live apart from him for ten months of the year?

She inhaled deeply, trying to calm her twittering insides.

Had she been wrong in thinking that he'd been enjoying his new relationship with Denise? She'd been sure he'd worked hard to attain the closeness they now shared. Why this sudden suggestion that Denise go to boarding school? she wondered.

Slipping her stockinged feet into azure pumps, Andrea pressed her hands against her midriff and took another deep breath.

How would he react to her probing the issue? That was the question that had caused her such turmoil. Her desire to see him, touch him, had wobbled on a rickety seesaw with the dread of their impending argument about his sending Denise away.

She tossed a deep blue scarf over one shoulder. The gossamer fabric floated down her back, and she fastened it at the belt of her pale yellow silk dress.

She'd thought that maybe she'd wait until another time to discuss the situation with him, hoping to spend this one evening without disagreements. But she knew she couldn't put it off. She'd promised Denise.

Besides, she knew what Denise was feeling. Andrea had spent most of her teenage years in a constant state of confusion because other people took it upon themselves to make decisions that concerned her and her life. Andrea's father was more guilty of this than anyone.

She remembered one particular occasion when she was just about Denise's age. Her father had been home for several weeks because he'd had the flu. When he'd found out that she'd been staying after school to attend Future Teachers of America meetings, he'd had a fit.

He'd told her there was no way he was going to let a child of his devote herself to one of the lowest-paying fields in the job market. He'd forced her to drop her membership in FTA, and he'd made her change her classes to a business-oriented curriculum.

After one year of college, she'd gotten her nerve up to tell him that teaching was what she wanted to do with her life. Again her father had had a fit, refusing to pay for her tuition if she persisted in studying education. But that hadn't daunted Andrea. She'd had to take a part-time job and several student loans to get her degree, but what she'd been most pleased about was the fact that she'd started making her own decisions, started being responsible for her own actions.

Those had been lean, lonely times, but she wouldn't change them for the world. Those experiences molded her into the person she was today. Everyone had to endure some bad moments in order to grow as a person. And this situation with Denise was, to the teenager at least, a very bad moment. If Andrea could smooth some of the roughest spots by talking to Ian, then she would.

The doorbell rang and Andrea heard Gunther's bark. She picked up her handbag on her way out of the bedroom and went to answer the door.

Her heart constricted at the sight of Ian. She feasted her eyes on the planes and angles of his handsome face. Her gaze dropped from his dark hair and eyes, not missing that little scar on the side of his chin, to his navy dinner jacket, crisp white shirt and dark tie, then lower still to his camel-colored trousers and oxblood loafers.

It wasn't until her gaze returned to his that she realized she'd been holding her breath.

"Hi." That one tiny word, slipping out with a rush of air, expressed every emotion she was feeling—pleasure, hungry passion, trepidation. She longed to throw her arms around him and tell him how much she'd missed him, but her anxiety tied her arms to her sides.

"May I come in?" he asked, his eyes twinkling with a teasing glint.

"Of course," she gushed, embarrassed that he perceived her longing.

She closed the door and turned to find herself wrapped in the warm cloak of his arms.

"I missed you," he whispered.

His spicy scent was heady, and she breathed deeply of it, letting the aroma conjure a multitude of intimate images in her head.

He leaned back and kissed her cheek.

"Miss me?"

She gave him a stiff little nod.

He chuckled.

"Andrea, what is it?" he asked, brushing his fingers along her jaw.

She shrugged out of his embrace.

"Nothing," she said. "I'm just not comfortable...."

He laughed outright this time and caught hold of her arm, running his hand up to cup her elbow.

If only he weren't so bent on touching me, she thought. The feel of his hands on her turned her skin into a tingling mass of nerves.

"You're not comfortable with what? This?" He pulled her to him and hugged her tight.

"Ian." She tried to wiggle away from him.

"Or this." He kissed her jaw and then her ear.

"Ian!" she squealed, struggling even more.

Gunther barked and Ian released his hold on Andrea.

"It's okay, boy," Andrea soothed the dog. "Go lie down."

"Andrea," Ian said, his voice soft with concern. "What is it?"

"It's nothing, really." She brushed her hair away from her face. "I want to talk, but we can do that over dinner.'' Lifting her eyes to his, she asked, "How was your trip? Did you get everything straightened out?''

"It was great,'' he said. "Two of the people who had been hurt are back to work already. The third is still in the hospital, but he's much better.''

"I'm glad,'' she said, smiling.

He reached for her again, sucking his breath in between clenched teeth. "I missed you, woman.'' He lifted her off her feet and twirled her in a tight circle.

She couldn't stop the laugh that bubbled inside her.

"I missed you, too,'' she admitted.

"I'm glad to hear that.'' He put her down and held her face between his hands. "Because you're going to be seeing a lot of me.''

Andrea's smile faded and she pulled away from him. She picked up her purse where she'd dropped it onto the chair.

"We'd better be going,'' she said, trying not to notice the frown creasing his brow.

She opened the door and stood waiting for him.

"What are you in the mood for?'' she asked.

One eyebrow raised provocatively and she was suddenly sorry she'd asked. But then he brightened and shouted, "Pasta!''

She shook her head and laughed.

Ian parked on Union Street, one of the busiest in Wilmington, two blocks from Andrea's favorite Italian restaurant. The rays of the setting sun gifted the city skyline with a blazing backdrop of fiery orange.

When Ian pushed open the door and ushered her inside, she smiled at the restaurant's homey interior and felt some of the tension melt from her shoulders.

En route to dinner, she'd babbled about how the human body converted food into energy. She realized it was only a vent for her anxiety. The incessant prattle was also something to focus on, something that dimmed her overwhelming urge to touch him.

When they were seated at a corner table, she watched Ian rest his elbow on the table and cradle his chin in his palm while she extolled the virtues of pasta.

"Pasta, potatoes, breads. There's no better food for a runner." Her words came in a rush. "People think they're fattening, but..." She stared at Ian's grin. "What is it?" she asked.

"I really hope there's something on your mind that's causing this intense biology lesson."

She felt her cheeks flame and was grateful that the dining room was dimly lit. Her eyes lowered, her fingers dropping to her lap to play with the deep red napkin that lay there.

"Andrea."

She lifted her eyes just enough to find the hand that had cupped his chin was now extended in a silent invitation.

And she answered it, sliding her fingertips over his, along the length of his fingers, over his palm and farther, until the fleshy part of her palm covered his wrist. Wrapping her fingers around it, she felt his pulse, warm and reassuring.

She watched his thumb draw lazy circles around her wrist bone and noticed how his tanned skin contrasted with her own. Her heart beat erratically, and she couldn't bring herself to look at him.

"Talk to me."

His voice was a silken appeal, and she lifted her chin to gaze into his dark eyes. She felt a wonderful sense of calm flow through her, as though she could tell him anything and he'd make it all right.

She opened her mouth to speak, but the waiter chose that moment to take their order.

Ian ordered an entrée and salad for them both at her nod of approval. He asked for a carafe of red house wine and then turned his full attention back to Andrea.

He must have noticed her hesitation because he said, "I was only gone for four days. What happened?"

She gave him a tiny smile, not knowing where to begin.

"It's about the surprise you brought Denise."

His face virtually lit up. "Did she tell you about it?" He leaned toward her in his excitement. "Andrea, I talked to the headmaster and toured the school. It's perfect. Denise'll get a good education *and* the best art instruction on the East Coast."

She watched his eyes dance, and he clasped her hand in both of his. Her wariness started to grow again.

"She'll be close enough that I could visit her often," he continued. "The location is perfect—skiing in the winter, horseback riding in the spring." He stared at her, beaming, waiting for a response.

How could she present Denise's case without snuffing out the flame of delight he'd built around this idea?

She squeezed his hand. "Ian . . ."

"She doesn't want to go?" His shoulders slumped and he frowned.

"It's not that she doesn't want to go," Andrea quickly assured him. "It's just..." Her voice trailed off again.

"For God's sake, what? Something's been bothering you all evening, spit it out."

She took a deep breath and decided to just dive in.

"When I was Denise's age, my father—"

"Robert." Ian spoke the name as though it left a bad taste in his mouth.

"Yes—" Andrea nodded "—Robert. He constantly made decisions for me without asking how I felt about them. By the time I had the guts to take the reins of my life out of his hands—" her eyes filled with deep emotion "—it was too late to bridge the chasm that had separated us. It's something I'll always regret."

He squeezed her hand. "Andrea, the chasm is never too wide to bridge." When she turned her head away, pointedly ignoring his statement, he sighed and returned to their original topic.

"So, Denise *did* tell you she doesn't want to go, and you're saying I shouldn't force her."

"That's not what I'm saying." She swiveled her head toward him, her eyes pleading with him to understand. "I only want you to talk to her, make sure this is something that *she* wants."

Ian shook his head in exasperation. "Why wouldn't she want it? Her education is important. And I want to give her the best I can."

"But...what's best isn't always...what's most expensive." Her words were spoken haltingly.

"I don't understand what you're trying to say here."
Ian slowly shook his head. "That's a damn good
school I want to send her to. And her painting is more
important to her than anything."

"Not as important to her as you are, as Harry is."

His face screwed up in confusion at her words.

"Ian, these weeks you've been home have meant so
much to Denise," she explained.

"And they've meant a lot to me, too. But this is the
way things are going to be from now on, my working
from home, I mean."

Andrea looked at him doubtfully.

"Andrea, when you first met me, you pointed out
some flaws in my relationship with my daughter." His
gaze was sharp, intense and held her spellbound.
"And I took immediate action to rectify those shortcomings. I'm letting Pamela do my traveling, I bought
an expensive computer and I put a second phone line
into the house. I can do everything from home now."

Andrea sat back, gently pulling her hands from his,
and stared at him. She hadn't realized to what lengths
he'd gone to improve his relationship with his family.
How could she have compared the man sitting before
her with the overbearing, uncaring man her father had
been? Ian's character was so far removed from her
father's that it made her wonder how she'd ever seen
a similarity to begin with.

"Denise's going to school in Connecticut isn't a decision that's been chiseled in stone. It's an option, a
choice. One that Denise and I will make together." He
smiled at her. "Don't worry, I'll talk to her."

"I'm sure you will," Andrea said softly. She picked up her fork and stabbed a sliver of red pepper from her salad plate, then raised her eyes to look at the man who'd just taken possession of her heart.

Chapter Nine

Andrea watched Ian and Denise stretching together and her heart swelled with happiness. During the weeks that the three of them had spent training, Andrea had witnessed father and daughter growing closer. It made her happy to see the radiant smile Denise was bestowing on her father at some humorous remark he'd just made.

Glancing out at the gathering crowd on the Market Street Mall, Andrea could see that the Wilmington Challenge was going to be well attended this year. She saw Harry up on the platform in deep conversation with the race's coordinator.

Her eyes darted back to Ian as he lifted his foot onto a concrete seat. And when he straightened his leg and bent forward to extend his calf muscle, she didn't fight the warm desire that began to grow inside her. The powerful muscles of his back rippled under the thin fabric of his white singlet. His maroon running shorts covered tight buttocks, and Andrea's gaze traveled appreciatively down the well-defined muscles of his legs.

These weeks of training had done wonderful things to Ian's body. He'd been trim and fit before, but the running had sculpted the muscles that now flexed under his sun-bronzed skin.

Ian's eyes found hers and he flashed her a grin that told her he was aware of her admiring scrutiny. Andrea couldn't help the heat that colored her cheeks.

It never ceased to amaze her how her feelings for Ian had changed since they'd met. That first afternoon at the school, she'd pegged him as an overbearing, domineering brute. She smiled at the memory, thinking she hadn't been too far off the mark. Ian *was* overbearing and domineering. But as she'd taken the time to get to know the man underneath the dynamic personality, she'd found he was also kind and caring, warm and witty, understanding and slow to anger, a trait that went well with her often misguided snap judgments.

The weeks they'd spent together made her realize that she *liked* the man that Ian was. She liked being with him, talking with him, sharing her life with him.

But she still couldn't shake the cloud of doubt that would sometimes fog her brain with wary questions. Would Ian want to continue their relationship after he'd finished the run today? Or did he think that their dating was just an extension of the business deal they'd made?

Andrea felt a heaviness in her chest as her heart constricted with trepidation. After he'd accomplished what he'd set out to prove by running this half marathon, would Ian revert into the man he'd been before she'd come into his life? Would the single-minded businessman who treated his family with cool aloofness reemerge? Andrea didn't know, but if he did, she wouldn't be the only person hurt. Denise would suffer tremendously at her father's reversion. So would Harry. Andrea shivered in spite of the hot August sun.

"Andrea?" Ian's voice brought her back to the milling crowd on the mall. "You look as though we've lost the race, and the starting gun hasn't even been fired yet."

Andrea smiled, pushing her gloomy speculations aside. "How are you feeling?"

"Nervous as a mouse in a cat's paw." Ian pulled her to him. "I need some reassurance."

Laying her head against his broad chest, she closed her eyes and wondered if this would be the last time she'd feel the security and warmth of his enfolding arms.

In the months they'd spent dating, Andrea had discovered that Ian was an extremely physical person, hugging her, touching her whenever he possibly could. And she'd quickly learned what any kind of contact with Ian did to her body. Finding herself enveloped by him now, she could feel the heat of desire kindling inside her at this very moment, building stronger with each passing second.

She took a deep breath and drew away from him. "You'll finish the run," she said. "What you lack in technique, you'll make up for in sheer determination."

Ian grinned. "I'm glad you have faith in me."

Forcing a weak smile, she swallowed the lump that formed in her throat. *If only I could have faith,* she thought.

Denise joined them and Andrea stepped away from Ian. "So, are you all limbered up?" she asked Denise.

"I think so, but my stomach feels upset."

"It's only nerves," Andrea told her. "Don't worry, you can do this. You both have one thirteen-mile run under your belts."

Andrea hated to bring up the long run the three of them completed the week before last. It had been tough and exhausting on both Ian and Denise, but they *had* finished, and Andrea felt impelled to remind them of that fact.

"Stay together," Andrea said, reiterating their strategy. "Maintain an eight-minute mile and take advantage of all the water stations. I don't want either of you dehydrating on me."

Denise nodded.

"Sure thing, Coach," Ian said, then he wrapped his arm around his daughter's shoulder, gazing down at her. "We're going to stick together, cross that finish line together. Right?"

Denise's face glowed. "You bet!"

Andrea's gloomy mood suddenly lifted as she watched this exchange, and she smiled brightly. Maybe everything would be okay. Maybe Ian wouldn't—

The race coordinator's voice cut into her thoughts as he called the runners to take their places behind the starting line. She watched father and daughter join the pack of runners, but then Ian broke away and trotted back toward her.

"What kind of coach are you, anyway?" he scolded teasingly. "You didn't wish me good luck."

"Oh," Andrea said, "by all means, good—"

Her well-wishing words were cut off as his lips covered hers. His kiss was warm and hungry, and a familiar churning excitement built inside her. But the kiss was over in a flash and as he ran back to the starting line, she recognized the deep disappointment that filled her.

"What have I done?" She mumbled the question aloud. *I've fallen in love.* The four simple words echoed in her mind.

But what kind of man was the real Ian Powers? Was he the dominating ogre that she'd first met? Or the compassionate, loving man she'd come to know?

The questions were still tumbling in her head as the starting gun was fired. She watched as Ian and Denise ran past.

"Don't bolt," she yelled, waving. "Keep a steady pace. You can do it!"

She kept them in sight until they turned the corner down the block and then she looked at her watch, calculating the time she'd need to be near the finish line to see them cross it.

Glancing up at the platform, she saw Harry talking to an older gentleman, and she walked over to them.

"Hi!" she called. "Can I come up and take a look at the trophies?"

The stranger conversing with Harry said, "I don't see why not," and bent to offer her his hand, pulling her onto the wooden deck.

"They're beautiful," she commented, letting her fingers brush the silver runner fixed to one of the two tallest trophies.

"Those are for the overall male and female winners," he said. "They certainly have changed from the trophies we won twenty-five years ago, eh, Harry?"

Harry grunted.

Andrea looked at the old man in the wheelchair, but couldn't discern whether her presence there upset him or not.

Ever since she'd asked Harry to help her track team and ended up laying her opinion on the line, he'd kept his distance. He'd come to every single track practice, but had watched Denise run from the other side of the fence. And Andrea hadn't seen him at all after school had let out in June.

"The trophies we won were about yea high." The man laughed, measuring the imaginary trophy between his hands.

Andrea nodded. "I saw Harry's."

"So, you know Harry Powers, the winner of the first Wilmington Challenge?" He clapped Harry on the shoulder. "I'm Jim Robbins." He stretched out his right hand. "I finished a second behind Harry."

"It was more like *thirty-two* seconds," Harry grumbled. "Jim, this is Andrea O'Connor. She coached my son and granddaughter for the race."

"So you're a runner." Jim nodded his approval, then said to Harry, "I could tell she's a runner. She has nice firm—"

"Okay, okay," Harry interrupted. "That's enough of that. Did you take an extra dose of Geritol this morning? You're old enough to be her father."

Jim laughed. "Just trying to give the little lady a compliment."

The race coordinator called Jim to the other end of the platform.

"Sorry about that," Harry said when they were alone.

"No problem. How have you been, Harry?" Andrea asked.

"Fine, fine." His words were terse.

She was wondering what she could say that might ease their relationship when her eyes caught the framed painting leaning against the table leg. She recognized it as the one Denise had shown her the evening of the picnic at Ian's. It had been completed, the metal trophy and shoe cleats gleaming from some unseen light source.

"Oh, Harry," she said. "It's lovely."

Harry only nodded.

She looked back down at the painting and then again at Harry, seeing the old man's eyes were misty with deep feeling.

"I'd wondered where those battered track shoes had gotten to," Harry said, forcing his words through his throat that was constricting with emotion. "That granddaughter of mine had swiped them to use as a model."

"She did a wonderful job." Andrea continued to study the painting, giving Harry a chance to fumble a handkerchief out of his pocket and wipe at his eyes.

"Andrea," he said after blowing his nose. "I know I can be a crotchety old man sometimes, and my behavior toward you has been atrocious." He waved her rebuttal aside with both hands. "Now, let me finish."

He stopped to clear his throat. "You've gone out of your way to help Ian and Denise so they could run this race. I want you to know I appreciate what you've done. I know you didn't want to train my son."

Andrea colored and lowered her eyes.

"I also know how stubborn he can be," Harry continued. "He told me all about how he had to force you into this whole mess. But don't hold it against him—he inherited that trait from me. I'm a stubborn old cuss, too."

A grin formed on Andrea's mouth and the urge to agree with him rose in her throat, but she stayed silent. But her smile froze with his next statement.

"He's also a born businessman. I've seen him go to any lengths in order to get a deal to go his way."

His comment caused a cloud of doubt to rain down on her, and a dark thought sprouted. Was wooing her part of the great lengths Ian had done to get her to train him? Pushing the fearful question aside, she concentrated on Harry's words.

Not noticing her uneasiness, Harry touched her arm and said, "I want you to know that I've taken your advice. I've been seeing a counselor. Talking things out." He straightened his shoulders with confidence. "It's taken me a long time, but I've realized that you didn't suggest I volunteer some time to the track team out of pity."

"I would never have done that," Andrea said.

"I know that now." Harry reached for her hand. "I'm sorry I ever thought you did. Can you forgive an old man?"

She smiled and squeezed his hand in answer.

"When September rolls around," he said, "I want to look your runners over. See if I could give 'em any helpful hints."

"Oh, Harry, I'm so glad." She let go of his hand to reach into her shoulder bag. Pulling out a scrap of paper and pencil, she scribbled dates and times. "But you won't have to wait until September." She laughed at his disconcerted look. "I hold a running camp every summer. We'll be meeting every other day until school starts."

She handed him the paper. "So, what do you say? Are those days good for you?"

Harry glanced at the information. "I'll be there," he said with conviction.

Jim hailed Harry from the table that held the trophies.

"I'd better go see what I can do over there," Harry said.

"Go ahead. I'm going to get myself something to drink." Andrea hopped down off the platform and went in search of some refreshment.

She was sipping from her bottle of cool orange juice when the first runner crossed the finish line one hour and eight minutes after the race had started. She knew she still had about half an hour before she needed to start looking for Ian and Denise, and she wondered how they were doing.

Runners trickled in for the next fifteen minutes and then they began to finish in small packs of four and five.

She watched as one young man collapsed and two volunteers pulled him to his feet. He needed to walk until he cooled down or he'd be hit with agonizing cramps.

Glancing down at her watch, she edged through the crowd on one side of the finish line. She craned her neck and looked up the road, but was overwhelmed by the number of runners advancing on the finish.

She ducked out of the crowd and went farther along the course, hoping to catch sight of Ian and Denise as they passed by.

When someone tapped her on the shoulder, she turned to see Ian's raven-haired business associate standing next to her. Pamela.

"You're Andrea O'Connor, aren't you?" the woman asked.

"Yes, I am," Andrea confirmed. "And you're Pamela."

"Pamela Jamison," she said. "We met..." Her voice trailed off, then she laughed. "Well, we almost met a few months ago."

"I remember," Andrea said. "And I really should apologize—"

"I won't hear of it." Pamela laughed again, an open and friendly laugh. "Ian can be exasperating at times. I enjoyed seeing you put him in his place."

"I never meant to...." Andrea mumbled.

"He was dumbfounded that evening at the restaurant," Pamela continued. "It was such fun seeing him at a loss for words. We had to break up our meeting and schedule another for the next day, he was so preoccupied. It was great."

Pamela's lightheartedness was infectious and Andrea found herself joining in.

"I have to admit I got a kick out of his expression when he turned and saw me standing over him." Andrea grinned at the memory.

Pamela looked down the street. "Has he finished yet?"

Andrea checked her watch. "He's a couple minutes behind schedule now. If everything's gone according to plan, he and Denise should be along soon."

But when two minutes passed and then two more, Andrea frowned. "I think I'll walk along the course and take a look for them."

She moved through the spectators, keeping her eyes on the runners. She spotted Denise running alone.

"Denise," Andrea called, moving onto the road to run beside Denise. "Where's your dad?"

"Back there," Denise said, panting, pointing behind her. "He's in trouble. He told me to go on."

"Are you okay?" Andrea asked.

Denise only nodded, conserving her energy.

"I'm going to find him," Andrea said.

Again Denise nodded.

Andrea knew she couldn't wade through the sea of runners, so she moved off the race course and ran along the sidewalk, dodging people as she went.

She met Ian about a quarter mile along the course. He was barely running, and he looked exhausted.

"Are you hurt?" she asked, pacing herself to his speed.

Ian eyes widened in surprise. "What are you doing here?"

"I'm coaching you," Andrea said. "Are you hurt?"

"Yes," he replied.

"Did you pull a muscle?"

"No, but everything hurts." He grimaced. "Every part of my body is screaming at me."

"That's normal," she assured him. "You can do this, Ian."

"That cobble-stone hill by the zoo wiped me out. I feel like I have no strength left."

He looked tired, but Andrea saw that his coloring was good. She reached out and touched his arm, feeling his warm, moist skin, and was pleased that he wasn't dry and clammy, a sure sign of dehydration. She said, "You might feel lousy, but don't focus on that. You look good, and I'm sure you can go on. Just take one step at a time. I'll stay with you."

"I'm not sure I can finish." His face was filled with tension.

"Of course, you can." But Andrea was aware that his pace was slowing with every step, and she knew he was throwing up a mental block about completing the run, rather than being physically unable to do it. "Ian, you've got to finish!"

He glared at her. "You did your job. You'll get your money," he retorted. "Now leave me alone."

They ran in silence. A frown creased Andrea's brow. She hadn't been thinking of the money. And she was sure he knew that. But the fact that he'd said it combined with the tone of his voice told Andrea the depth of anguish and defeat he was feeling.

She wanted him to finish the race for his sake, and she had to think of some way she could help him find the resources to do it.

Her lips slid into a sly grin as she thought of the perfect solution. She quickly hid her smile and waited.

When Ian's pace slowed again, she quickened hers just a bit.

"Quitter!" she called over her shoulder.

Ian lengthened his stride to catch up with her. "What did you call me?"

"A quitter," she repeated. "I told you the first day we met that you didn't have what it would take."

Ian's mouth set in an angry frown.

"I've wasted four months of my time on you."

His lips thinned.

"And now you're going to quit with only a half mile to go."

Andrea watched with pleasure as Ian's jaw muscle contracted. She knew she had to whip him into a fury if he was going to forget his misery and complete the run.

"I *knew* I could have bet my best pair of running shoes that you'd never do it."

He glared at the pavement in front of his feet for several steps before turning his thunderous eyes toward Andrea. "You made that same bet the day I met you. Do you remember? I couldn't have won then because the odds were in your favor. But this time—" Ian picked up his pace. "This time I'm going to collect!" he bellowed at her over his shoulder.

Andrea ran off the race course and stopped, slapping her hand over her mouth to keep her laughter from escaping.

By the time Andrea arrived at the finish line, she found Harry and Pamela sitting with Denise, who was sucking on a thick, juicy orange slice next to the awards platform.

"Hi!" she called to them. "Congratulations, Denise." She gave the teenager a quick hug.

"Thanks. I feel so good!" Denise exclaimed. "I was afraid I wouldn't be able to finish."

"But you did," Harry said, his eyes full of pride as he beamed at his granddaughter.

Andrea looked at Pamela. "Did you see Ian come in?"

"Yes, and did he ever look stormy."

"I thought you'd be running with him," Denise said to Andrea.

"I didn't have to," Andrea said. "I knew if I made him angry enough, he'd finish on his own." Andrea grinned. "I called him a quitter."

Pamela gave an unladylike snort, and Denise giggled.

"No wonder he looked so angry." Harry chuckled.

"You hit him below the belt with that one, Andrea," Pamela said, laughing.

"But he needed it," Denise commented. "He was going to give up."

"Well, you're right, then." Pamela ruffled Denise's hair. "He needed it."

"Where is he, by the way?" Andrea scanned the crowd.

"He grabbed a banana and a cup of water and headed for the car," Pamela said. "He was going to get some dry clothes and use the shower facilities at the YMCA."

"The information leaflet said the showers would only be available to the runners for two hours," Denise said, sliding off the low wall where she'd been sitting. "So, I'm going to go grab a quick shower, too."

"You need it," Harry teased, wrinkling his nose.

"Oh, Pops!"

Andrea watched Denise trot off and turned back toward Pamela and Harry.

"Was Ian really angry?" she asked.

"Positively livid." Pamela eyes were bright. "But he'll get over it. He'll understand what you did and why."

"I hope so."

The three looked at one another, and they burst out laughing again.

"I guess this means I owe you some money," Pamela said.

Andrea's laughter waned. "What are you talking about?"

Pamela rummaged in her purse, extracting her checkbook as she explained, "I bet Ian that he couldn't finish the run." She began to make out the check. "If he didn't finish, he'd have had to give me a raise. Now that he *has* finished, I have to make your school a donation." She signed her name and ripped off the check, handing it to Andrea. "Something about track equipment you need."

Harry slapped his thigh. "Ha, ha! See there? I told you my son was a born businessman." He shook his head in wonder. "Now, not only did he get expert training, but he's also saved himself a bunch of money."

Andrea stared at the blue slip of paper in her hand until the numbers and letters blurred together. The blood rushed to her head, making a whooshing noise in her ears, and she felt light-headed and faint.

Could it really be possible that Ian wasn't going to fulfill his end of their bargain? She'd worked for four long months, giving him the best coaching she knew how, and now Ian's father was telling her that he'd contrived a way to get Pamela to pay his debt. The thought was staggering. She'd come to trust him. How could he let her down so? Her mouth went dry and her stomach felt suddenly queazy.

But hadn't there been a shadow of suspicion coiled in the back of her mind all along, just waiting to be sprung?

Harry's laughter shook her out of the fog she was in. "The deals Ian cooks up," he commented, "never cease to amaze me!"

Andrea abruptly turned and walked up the street toward the red brick building where she knew Ian was. She didn't see the people who were talking animatedly about the strategies they'd used to finish the race; she didn't hear their personal-record stories. She wasn't even aware when Harry called over the loudspeaker that the postrace ceremonies were about to begin.

She had the promised money. The check was right here in her hand. But the money wasn't the issue. The source was. She and Ian had made a bargain; Ian would donate a set sum of money in exchange for her coaching services.

Hadn't she completed her part? Hadn't she given him a crash course in the sport of running? Hadn't she seen to it that he was trained well enough to finish the Wilmington Challenge?

A blazing hot anger filled her as she answered a resounding yes to each question.

Where then did he get off thinking that he could get someone else to pay his dues?

She stopped in the middle of the sidewalk. But wasn't that exactly the kind of thing her father would have done? Getting something for nothing was the ultimate deal to a driven businessman. And wasn't that just what Ian was? A died-in-the-wool driven businessman? Harry had said it. So had Denise. And Pamela must realize it, too. The woman had good-naturedly paid out Ian's donation as though it hadn't been the first time she'd been bested by Ian. And, if Andrea had been smart enough to obey her instincts, she would have recognized it, too.

Oh, but he'd come so close to blinding her with his kind words, gentle embraces and hungry kisses. She'd all but fallen for it, too. Why had she let her physical feelings and emotions get in the way of what she'd known to be the truth? Way hadn't she paid more attention to that shadowy doubt that hovered over her every time she'd even thought of him?

Her chin quivered, and her sight blurred with unshed tears. Now she knew that what she'd feared most was going to come true. Ian's life-style was so ingrained that despite their attraction to each other, he was going to revert to what he'd been when they'd first met. His reneging on his end of their bargain told her that the turnabout had already begun. And she had no room in her life for a man like that. No matter how much she'd come to love him.

She turned the corner and walked right into him.

"Whoa, there," he said. "Where are you going?"

"To find you."

"Well, here I am." He grasped her upper arm, oblivious to the chaos rioting inside her. "I could use something to drink," he said. "Let me buy you something."

"I don't want anything."

Confused by her tone, Ian shrugged and went up to a street vender, got a soda and took a long swallow.

"Ian," she said, her voice belligerent.

"Wait a minute, Andrea. I have something I need to say." He ran his hand through his still-damp hair. "I know that you said those things out there during the race so I'd get angry enough to finish." He grinned. "It worked. Thanks. I probably would have given up without you."

"Don't thank me yet." She spat the words at him through clenched teeth. "Pamela told me about the deal the two of you made. Wheeling and dealing. That's what you do best, isn't it, Ian?"

His smile faded. "It was supposed to be a surprise."

"Some surprise!" Her eyes narrowed. "I'd think you wouldn't have wanted me to find out at all."

His words and the frown on his forehead didn't register with her, and she plunged ahead. "But getting a free ride is all that's important to the high and mighty Ian Powers."

His expression clouded and his jaw set. "Be careful, Andrea."

"Free ride," she repeated defiantly. "I worked my tail end off to get you ready for this race. I personally supervised each and every phase of your training. I molded that pitiful body of yours into the conditioned runner that you are today."

"Andrea—"

His tone was a warning, but she went on, heedless. "And what do I get for all the time and effort I put into this whole affair? I get rooked by the very person I tried to help." She glared up at him. "But I guess I should be proud to have been burned by the best. Huh, Ian? You've scorched me worse than my own father ever did."

Ian's eyes narrowed and his quiet voice held an underlying current when he assured her, "You're going to get your money."

"But it's not your money, is it, Ian? You don't even have the decency to pay your own debt." She batted her hair out of her eyes. "You've schemed a way to have Pamela pay it for you!"

The muscles in his face contorted in anger. "You don't know what you're talking about."

"I know exactly what I'm talking about." She glanced at the check she clutched between her fingers and impulsively shoved it at him. "I don't want Pamela's money."

"Andrea," he said, ignoring the check and clutching her shoulder.

She shrugged out of his grasp. "Don't touch me!" Her voice was cold as she pushed Pamela's payment at him. "Take it, Ian. I don't want it!"

His jaw snapped shut and his nostrils flared with fury, but he calmly plucked the check from her hand. "That flaw in your character that makes you dive into things headfirst isn't cute anymore, Andrea. In fact, I think it's just caused you to snap that pretty little neck of yours. You've jumped to the wrong conclusion once too often.''

He turned and strode off toward the crowd.

Andrea watched him go, hearing Harry's faint voice announcing the names of the winners. She let her tears flow freely now that Ian wasn't there to see them. Then she did the only thing she could. She turned in the opposite direction and ran.

Chapter Ten

Andrea stood in her backyard, mechanically throwing the mangled tennis ball that Gunther kept fetching and dropping at her feet.

She'd come home over three hours ago, showered, changed and done a multitude of mindless chores, trying to keep thoughts of Ian at bay. But no amount of cleaning and straightening could erase the bitter scene that kept playing through her head.

She wasn't a coward and didn't usually feel the need to escape from difficult situations. But that Ian had walked away from her as though *he* were the one who had been wronged had been more than she could stand. So, she'd run away from him and his hurtful words. The whole rotten mess stank to high heaven.

Ian hadn't planned on making the promised donation. Probably from the very beginning he'd been scheming one way or another to get out of it. She should be thankful for the way things had turned out. If she hadn't spoken with Pamela, she might have never known—she might have really gotten burned.

A wave of depression washed over her as she thought of the fact that now she would have no money—not Ian's, not Pamela's, nor any from the school's budget—to use in purchasing new equipment for her students. She'd gone through all this for nothing. Mr. Scott might even fire her when he heard the outcome.

Returning Pamela's money had been childish, she knew that. But the thought of keeping the check rankled her so badly she couldn't help refusing it.

Andrea looked up to see Gunther sniffing at one corner of the fence, the ball forgotten. She sat on the wooden steps and rested her chin in her palm.

She wished she had followed her first instincts where Ian was concerned. She wished she hadn't let his honeyed words color her perception of him. But she had. She'd gone further still, falling head over heels in love with the man.

She'd gone out on a limb for Ian Powers, and it had snapped under the weight of her emotions. She shouldn't have let herself get so involved with him, but since she had, she'd just have to pay the price for her mistakes.

Part of that price included the gloom that now filled her to the brim. She snatched up a pebble lying at her feet and hurled it out into the yard.

How long would she hurt? How long before the scars on her heart began to heal? How long would it be before Ian's name ceased to conjure images of warm passion?

When the doorbell rang, Andrea hopped up, brushing off the back of her shorts. Gunther bounded through the porch door when she opened it and ran, barking, toward the living room.

"Gunther, sit!" Andrea waited for the German shepherd to obey her command before she pulled open the door.

Ian's stoney expression greeted her.

She didn't even try to hide the irritation that welled up inside her. "What do you want?"

"Just came to collect," he said, brushing past her to stalk to the center of the room before turning to face her. "You made a bet. I'm here for the shoes."

Andrea swallowed and gripped the brass door handle as though it was her lifeline. Her heart ached at the sight of him. Why couldn't he just leave her alone with her misery? Why did he find it necessary to torture her?

"Ian, I don't want you here," she cried, fighting the tears that threatened to spill.

He whirled around to face her. "I don't care what you want! You're going to listen to what I have to say."

All the frustration and anger and hurt she'd felt since she'd run from Ian earlier rose to the surface, forcing a vent for itself. She slammed the door, her fists clenched at her sides.

"I knew the kind of person you were the first time I laid eyes on you," she said, restraining the words from coming too fast. "I *knew* you were just like my father, an overbearing tyrant, not caring what anyone else might think or want. Hearing you say the words has done me a world of good."

She stepped behind the couch and splayed her fingers on its headrest, willing herself to relax. "My father can't dictate to me any longer, Ian. And neither can you." She raised her chin. "I don't have to listen to anything you have to say."

His hard mouth wasn't softened by the cold, slow smile that curved his lips. "But you do, Andrea." He shook his head, his eyes full of scorn. "When are you going to open your eyes and see what's in front of you. Look at you. Look at where you've chosen to position yourself for protection." He indicated the couch with a curt jerk of his head. "Andrea, it's not me you need protection from. It's your own passionate emotions that you're trying to hide from."

"That's ridiculous!" The words dripped contempt and Andrea felt the heat of anger flush her face. "The only emotion I feel toward you is hate. And I feel it with a passion."

His chuckle was humorless. "There's a fine thread that separates love and hate."

"What are you saying?" Her eyes were wide with incredulity. "You think I—"

"I'm reserving comment," he interrupted. "I won't tell you what you feel. You'll have to figure that out for yourself."

"I can't believe my ears! The great and powerful Ian Powers is passing up a chance to tell me what I feel." She shook her head sarcastically. "That's so out of character, Ian. My father would be so disappointed."

"I'm sick and tired of hearing you complain about your father." Ian planted one hand squarely on his hip. "From what I've gleaned, he was a man who loved his daughter the best way he knew how—by providing for her and trying to steer her in the right directions in life. Your father loved you, Andrea. You're just too damned stubborn to see it." Ian pointed his finger at her. "He just wasn't lucky enough to have someone point out that his child needed a relationship with him more than she needed the things his hard-earned money provided. But it's very low of you to hold that against him."

Stepping toward her, in a low, tight voice he said, "You've thrown challenges at me from day one, Andrea. And I've met them time and again. Well, I have a challenge for you now. I think you should contact your father. Talk to him." He leaned forward. "Communicate with him. Try to work out some of the anger you feel, because it's making you jump to hasty conclusions and it's coloring your perception of the most important aspect of your life."

He took another step toward her, his tone softening as he said, "You saw problems between my daughter and me and you helped us work them out. For that I'll be eternally grateful. But I wish like hell you were perceptive enough to see the mistake you're making right now."

Silence and anger separated them. They stood glaring at each other.

Andrea searched his hard features for a clue to his last statement. But before she had a chance to figure it out, he erased all emotion from his face, his shoulders slumping a fraction.

"Like I said when I first arrived, I only came to collect." He pushed his fists into his pockets.

"You're not really serious."

"I'm serious." He extended one hand toward her, waving his fingers in a "gimme" motion.

She stood firm. "What in the world are you going to do with my shoes?"

"Keep them," he told her. "It'll teach you a small lesson—don't kick a man when he's down."

"I didn't kick you," she snapped. "I only prodded you a little."

"Anyway, I didn't finish the race in time to win a trophy. I need something to set on my shelf and admire, something to commemorate my accomplishment."

Andrea glared at him. "You just want to rub my nose in it." She bent and slipped off one of her running shoes. She tossed it at him and was pleased when it thumped him on the chest before he caught it. She pulled the other shoe off and hurled it at him, but he snatched it in midair.

He gave her a nod and a cocky smile and headed toward the door. He stopped short and turned to face her.

"I almost forgot," he said, reaching into his back pocket. He extended a white envelope to her. "This is for you."

She stepped from around the couch, her bare feet making her feel utterly naked. She frowned and looked at the envelope, making no move to accept it.

"Go on, take it," he said, then added wryly, "I think you'll be pleased."

When she took the envelope a smug question passed through her mind. Had she made Ian feel so bad that he'd decided to pay her the money he owed? Well, he should feel bad, and he should pay his debt.

"Pamela's hosting a celebration dinner for us to-night at her apartment. Her address is on the front, there."

"But, Ian, I can't—"

"You can. And you will." Her eyes narrowed. "If you won't do it for me, you'll do it for my dad and Denise. My father told me he'd agreed to help coach your track team, and Denise dedicated herself to training for the run today. They deserve some recognition. If you're not there by eight, I'll be back to throw you over my shoulder and carry you there."

After he left, Andrea stared at the door, knowing his threat wasn't an idle one. He'd be back if she didn't show up at Pamela's.

Well, she'd go to the dinner. Not because she was frightened of Ian's warning, but for Denise and Harry. Denise had worked hard all spring to train for the half marathon, and Harry had become Andrea's friend. Andrea wanted to explain to Pamela why she hadn't accepted her check. Some fresh-cut flowers might help to soften the explanation.

Andrea reached into the envelope and was surprised when she pulled out not one, but two checks: the original check signed by Pamela Jamison, the other carrying Ian's bold signature. Each check was made out for the amount that she and Ian had agreed on, leaving Andrea with double the donation she'd been expecting.

What was this all about? Andrea stared at the two checks, pondering the question.

She remembered her angry accusation earlier, when she'd railed against Ian for letting Pamela pay his debt. She'd obviously made him feel guilty enough that he'd decided to make his promised donation. But why, then, was Pamela's check included?

As Andrea gazed down at her bare toes, her jaw slowly clenched with the realization that Ian simply wanted to avoid the embarrassment of returning Pamela's check.

"Oh, Ian," Andrea whispered aloud.

Andrea had been soaking in the tub for half an hour. She'd pushed all thoughts about the two checks aside, feeling undecided about what to do about them. She focused her attention instead on Ian's summation concerning her father.

Your father loved you the best way he knew how. Ian's words replayed themselves in her mind. Was it possible that her father *did* love her?

She lifted herself out of the now chilly water and wrapped a towel around her body, tucking one corner between her breasts. She sloshed out of the bathroom, unconscious of the fact that she was still dripping wet. Rummaging through the bookcase in her bedroom, she found the dusty old photo album she was looking for.

The yellowed pages crackled as she opened them. The black-and-white pictures were creased and delicate. Images of her smiling father stared up at her. One picture had been taken as her father held her, laughing, atop a white pony, another as they rode a giant merry-go-round at a carnival.

There weren't many pictures, but in every one, her father's expression was the same—he looked at his only daughter with love and adoration.

Andrea studied the prints for a long time. Her father did love her. The proof was there in black-and-white. Happy memories of when she was very young flooded her brain, further evidence that, at one time, she had returned that love.

But when had everything turned sour between them? Had it been when he'd been forced to take that new job and had to travel? Or had it been when she'd hit rebellious adolescence?

She stared off, wondering how both of them could have let their relationship get into the lousy shape it was in. She glanced at the telephone on the night-stand. Would a call to Kansas start a rebuilding of her and her father's lost relationship? She closed the album and went to sit on the edge of the bed, lifting the phone receiver from its cradle. She could only try. The last thought that flashed through her mind as she heard the ring on the other end of the line was that she was taking Ian up on his challenge.

Andrea parked her car and hurried up the steps of Pamela's apartment building. She was late and her heart was racing.

She pressed the buzzer and waited. She didn't know what this evening had in store. Even though she was hurt and angry with Ian, she had to remember that he'd inadvertently been responsible for her and her father's budding understanding. Ian's enlightening words had been like a huge hammer that chipped away at the wall between her and her father, and she wanted to thank him for making her see how wrong she'd been.

With that in mind, she'd decided to keep Pamela's check and let Ian's secret remain just that, a secret. That way, Highland Academy would get the extra money for the equipment and Ian and Pamela's business relationship wouldn't be jeopardized.

Pamela opened the door. "Hi," she said. "I'm glad you could come."

Andrea handed her the bouquet of spider mums, roses and daisies. "Thank you for inviting me."

"Everybody's in there," Pamela said, ushering her through the foyer. "I'm going to put these in water." She buried her nose in the beautiful blooms and went off toward the kitchen.

Ian met Andrea at the living room doorway, and the sight of him filled her with an odd array of emotions. She was angry that she'd had to goad him into making his promised donation. She was afraid that they might spoil the party with another quarrel. Yet, at the same time, her heart was bursting with the happy news about her conversation with her father, and she felt the need to tell Ian. And woven among all these feelings was that same steady rhythm of desire that sang through her every time she was near him.

"I'm glad you decided to show up," Ian said. "I was about ready to come get you."

"There was no need for that." Her words were clipped by her nervous tension. "Ian, you don't have to worry. I plan to keep your secret."

"What secret?" he asked. "What are you talking about?"

"The—"

"Miss O'Connor," Denise called from across the room, "look what I won!"

Denise ran over and handed Andrea a small trophy, a replica of the one Harry received at the first Wilmington Challenge.

"I took third place in my age division," Denise told her.

"That's wonderful, Denise." Andrea ran her eyes over the trophy with pride, turning it around in her hands. She looked up at the teenager. "I saw the painting you did for your grandfather. It's perfect."

"I'm so proud of that girl." Harry's smile lit up his wrinkled face.

Andrea smiled a greeting at the old man. "I am, too," she said.

"The same goes for me." Ian gave his daughter a quick hug.

"Did Ian offer you a drink?" Pamela asked Andrea when she returned from the kitchen.

"No, but I'd like one, please." Andrea followed the woman over to the small bar. "Pamela, I want to thank you for the donation you made to the school. It was very generous."

"It was for a good cause." Then Pamela grinned. "It would have been much more fun to get another raise out of Ian, but—" she shrugged "—that's the way the mop flops."

As Pamela handed Andrea a glass of white wine, the timer sounded in the kitchen.

"Oops, the lasagna's ready to come out of the oven. Excuse me just a minute." Pamela disappeared again.

Andrea turned and saw Ian sitting at the opposite end of the room, staring at her. She avoided him, joining Denise and Harry as the two of them discussed the race.

"I thought I was going to pass out," Denise said.

"But you didn't," Harry commented. "You kept right on running until you crossed that finish line."

Denise shook her head and looked up at Andrea. "That last mile was a killer."

Andrea chuckled. "It always is."

Harry nodded knowingly, then shot a question across the room at his son. "How about you, Ian? How do you feel about finishing the Wilmington Challenge?"

"I feel really good about it."

"Good enough to take the challenge again next year?" Harry raised his eyebrows.

Ian shook his head, and Harry laughed.

"I plan to stick with the running," Ian said. "But only short distances. To keep myself fit." Ian moved to the bar and set down his empty glass, then looked directly at Andrea. "I'm not cut out for those long runs, but I'd hate for my body to regress to the pitiful shape it was in before Andrea found me."

Andrea's cheeks flamed.

"I have something for you," Denise said to Andrea, presenting her with a small painting.

Andrea remembered the mauve-and-pink flowers depicted on the canvas as the painting she'd admired in Denise's studio.

"I thought you were going to sell it," Andrea said.

"I changed my mind." Denise handed her the framed painting. "I want you to have it. You've done so much for me—training me for the run, talking to Dad about the school."

At the mention of the boarding school, Andrea looked at Denise questioningly.

"Dad and I have compromised." Denise smiled. "We won't make a decision until we've seen the school together. We're going to Connecticut next weekend."

"I'm glad," Andrea said.

"Are you disappointed that I didn't pack her bags and ship her off, handcuffed?" Ian's dark eyes bored into her.

Again Andrea felt heat color her face. *Why is he taunting me?* she wondered.

"Dinner's ready."

The four of them followed Pamela's summons into the dining area. A chair had been removed from one end of the table to allow Harry easier access. Pamela sat at the other end, Denise beside her father, which left Andrea to sit facing Ian.

The gooey lasagna was delicious and the aroma of the garlic bread made Andrea's mouth water.

But her appetite didn't last long as Ian took full advantage of the first lull in the conversation. He put down his glass of water with meticulous care and pierced Andrea with his gaze.

"So," he said, his voice low and mischievous. "What are you going to do with all that money?"

Andrea stopped chewing and lowered her eyes. Why had he brought up the subject? She'd thought he would have avoided it like the plague. He must be thoroughly disgusted with her and the fact that she'd made him feel guilty enough to write that check. Well, he couldn't make her feel bad about taking his money. It was money that he'd promised, money the school needed. She deserved that money.

She eyed him boldly. "I'm going to buy gym equipment with it. Lots of gym equipment."

"Were you surprised when you opened the envelope?" Denise asked. "Dad's been excited for weeks about his great surprise. He knew you needed more money than what he could afford to give, so he egged Pamela into making that little bet." She giggled. "He knew he could win all along."

Andrea stopped chewing and looked at Denise, then her gaze swung back to Ian. His eyebrows rose in a mocking gesture, and his slight nod made the color slowly drain from her face. She swallowed the lump of cheese that was stuck in her throat.

Oh, my God! The words echoed in her head so loudly she was afraid she'd uttered them aloud. What had she done?

Ian had never meant to get out of paying the money. She inhaled, letting the thought sink in. Suddenly, the clouds in her brain parted and Ian's comforting words the night of the PTA meeting came floating back to her. He'd told her that things would work out. He'd insinuated then that she would get the money she needed.

She'd thought that he was only consoling her. But he'd been planning all along to get the additional money needed for the equipment. He'd gotten Pamela to make a donation so Andrea would have double the amount of money.

"I was very surprised," she admitted to Denise. She glanced at Ian and said softly, "I wish you would have told me, Ian."

"But it was a surprise," Denise explained simply. "Only Dad and I knew."

Andrea gave Denise a weak smile. "And it was a nice surprise."

She lowered her eyes to her plate again and picked up her fork to toy with her food. She stuck a small crust of bread into her mouth, but it didn't fill the emptiness that consumed her as she realized the horrible mistake she'd made. Over and over again she'd misconstrued Ian's motives. Over and over again she'd misjudged him. How could she ever find the words to apologize?

"How nice was my little surprise?"

Ian's taunting question made her choke on the bite of bread she'd just swallowed. She grabbed for her goblet of water and gulped.

"Now don't ride her, Ian," Harry chided his son. "You had me fooled, too. I thought you'd finagled your way out of paying up even after all the expert training Andrea gave you."

"She certainly did give me expert training, Dad," Ian said.

"Yes," Pamela agreed. "And Andrea should be awarded a medal of honor just for taking you on."

"That's true," Ian responded, but the look in his eyes told Andrea that he thought she should be choking on a plateful of crow feathers rather than the delicious meal Pamela had prepared. Andrea knew from the glint in his eyes that he was playing with her, and she deserved everything he dished out.

When they'd finished eating, the Powers family retired to the living room while Pamela and Andrea cleared the table.

Andrea stood at the sink, rinsing dishes and handing them to Pamela, who stacked them in the dishwasher.

"I don't know what's eating Ian," Pamela commented. "He's positively brooding."

Andrea took a deep breath. "It's me."

"I thought so." Pamela smiled at her. "You've kept him in turmoil since he first met you."

"What?"

Pamela's light laughter tinkled like a wind chime. "I knew from the moment I saw you that you'd give Ian a run for his money." She looked up at Andrea. "Pardon the pun."

Rinsing the remaining dishes in silence, Andrea thought of all the times Ian had tried to get close to her only to have her push him away. She'd let the doubt that was crouched in the corner of her mind keep her from believing in him. And his mocking behavior toward her this evening told her that nothing she could say or do would make things right again.

But she had to at least let him know what he'd done for her and her father. She had to tell him of the wonderful turn of events that he'd put into motion.

"I need to speak with Ian," she told Pamela, drying her hands on a tea towel.

She went into the living room and saw only Harry and Denise. "Where's Ian?"

"Out there." Harry pointed toward the French doors that led to the balcony.

Andrea followed his direction, skirting the table where they'd just eaten, and slid open the glass door.

Ian stood at the railing and didn't even turn when she stepped outside and slid the door closed.

She stood there a moment, looking at his back, as she wondered how to begin.

"Ian," she said.

He turned and glanced at her before returning his gaze to the horizon.

"Ian, I'd like to talk with you." She went to stand beside him, grasping the wrought-iron barrier with both hands.

"So, talk," he said.

"Ian—" she inhaled deeply "—I've been wrong."

He turned his head toward her, one eyebrow lifted. "Oh?" The word was filled with sarcasm.

"About my father."

"Oh." His facial muscles relaxed.

"I wanted you to know that I called him."

Ian nodded. "I'm glad," he said, turning his stony expression toward the city skyline.

"We talked for over an hour." She brushed her hair behind her ear. "That's why I was late." Her mouth was dry as she tried to find the words to express how she felt. "Ian, we talked. Really talked. For the first time in years."

"That's nice, Andrea. I'm happy for you." Ian stood, unmoving, like a cold marble statue.

Andrea placed her hand on his forearm. "I have you to thank for that," she said.

"You're welcome, Andrea."

She couldn't be sure, but she thought she saw the hard look in his eyes soften a little.

"It was good to hear my father's voice," she told him. "We didn't do much to break down the wall between us, but we've started and that's what counts. He's coming to visit."

She smiled at Ian and was rewarded when he smiled back.

Brushing at her hair again, she said, "You were right about my father. And some other things, too."

He turned his body toward her, his hip resting on the railing.

She lifted her hand and smoothed it down along the lapel of his jacket. "You were right about my being frightened of my emotions. I was." She let her gaze drop. "I am."

Ian stood stock still, and she let her hand drop to her side.

"You were right about what was between us," she said, tilting her head. "It was there, strong, alive. I felt it from the very beginning." She hesitated. "But I've messed everything up...."

Ian's chest expanded as he took a deep breath. "I was so hurt today hearing what you thought of me, how low you thought I'd stoop."

Andrea's eyes misted with understanding. "I know, and I'm so sorry. You were also right when you said I let my feeling about my father color—" she hesitated "—the most important thing in my life." She searched his eyes, hoping he understood all that she was feeling. "Ian, my faith in you was like a big, leaky bucket. Every time I filled it up, it somehow drained empty again."

"I knew that the hole in that bucket of yours were your memories of your father," he told her. "Every time you compared the two of us, the holes only became bigger." He studied her face. "But, now that you've started talking to your dad, I'm sure you'll be able to plug those holes."

"I promise you, I'll work hard at it."

Ian lowered his gaze. "But you aren't the only one who messed things up." He took hold of her wrist. "I'm guilty, too." Shaking his head, he laughed harshly. "And all because I wanted to surprise you."

Then he gave her a rueful smile as he tried to explain. "The night of the home-school meeting at Highland, you were so damned disappointed about the board cutting your allowance out of the budget. I wanted to find some way to get you what you needed."

"I know that now, Ian." A single tear slid down her cheek. It was joined by another as she was once again engulfed by the feeling that she'd wronged him. "And I thought you were trying to avoid your end of our bargain."

"I should have told you," he said, his taut expression full of regret. "I should have known better than to spring a surprise on someone who jumps into everything headfirst."

"I'm sorry about that, too."

"Don't be," he told her, tipping up her chin with his fingers and wiping away a tear with the pad of his thumb. "That's one of the things that makes you so irresistible."

She rested her hand on his shoulder and gazed up at him sadly. "If only things had turned out differently."

"Why do you say that?" he asked, moving close and pulling her into his arms.

She lifted her questioning eyes to his.

"We've already made all the mistakes," he said. "Let's just hope we've learned from them." Then he grinned. "You can bet I'll never throw you a surprise party."

She was suddenly filled with a radiant happiness when she realized just what he was saying. Her lips tipped up in a tentative smile and after an apprehensive pause, she slipped her arms around his neck. "You can bet I'll never compare you to anyone else. Ever," she promised. Then she lifted her glinting eyes to his and said, "And I'll never prod you when you're down."

"Prod? You kicked me, woman," he growled teasingly. "I still have the bruises to show for it."

She laughed softly and pressed her body against him, her heart swelling with happiness at knowing they were getting a second chance. "I should have come barefoot tonight as penance."

It was his turn to laugh, and he kissed the tracks of her tears dry. "I wish you had," he whispered. "Then I would have given you my gift earlier."

"A gift?" Andrea loved presents and couldn't hide her pleasure. "I love you," she whispered, planting a kiss on his firm chin.

"I know it's a surprise, but don't beat me over the head with it." He picked up the box off the glass-topped patio table and handed it to her. "After our talk this afternoon, I thought there was no way you'd accept it."

"Oh, Ian." She smiled, ripping open the bright wrapping paper. "It's a pair of running shoes, isn't it?"

"A replacement," he said.

She lifted the lid off the box and pulled out the white running shoes, a pair identical to the ones he'd taken from her earlier.

"They're perfect! Thank you, Ian."

A flash of green caught her eye and she looked more closely at the shoes. Tied in the middle of one of the bows, a square-cut emerald flanked by two triangular-shaped diamonds glittered at her.

"Ian," she breathed, "it's beautiful."

"I thought I knew how you felt about us even though you were saying the exact opposite. It was a big risk," he said, grinning. "But taking risks is what any businessman worth his salt does."

Untying the shoelaces, he slipped the ring on her finger and asked, "So how about it? Will you run through life with me?"

Tears filled her eyes once more. But these were enchanted tears of rapture as an unspeakable joy flowed through her. She reached up on tiptoe to kiss his lips and then she smiled. "I'd love to." Her smile widened as she added, "We'll stick to short distances, so you can keep up."

He laughed and kissed her, a fierce, fevered kiss that lasted until they were both breathless. "Andrea, my love," he said, "with you beside me, I could run to the ends of the earth."

* * * * *

Silhouette Romance®

LONG, TALL TEXANS

HARDEN
Diana Palmer

In her bestselling LONG, TALL TEXANS series, Diana Palmer brought you to Jacobsville and introduced you to the rough and rugged ranchers who call the town home. Now, hot and dusty Jacobsville promises to get even hotter when hard-hearted, woman-hating rancher Harden Tremayne has to reckon with the lovely Miranda Warren.

The LONG, TALL TEXANS series continues! Don't miss HARDEN by Diana Palmer in March...only from Silhouette Romance.

LTT-1

WRITTEN IN THE STARS

Will The Pisces Man Be Lured Into Romance?

Find out in March with FOR HEAVEN'S SAKE by Brenda Trent . . . the third book in our WRITTEN IN THE STARS series!

There was only one fish in the sea for pet groomer Kelly-Ann Keernan—she'd fallen for sexy Steve Jamison, hook, line and sinker! But will the private Pisces man ever say goodbye to bachelorhood and hello to married bliss?

Be sure to catch the passionate Pisces man's story, FOR HEAVEN'S SAKE by Brenda Trent . . . only from Silhouette Romance!

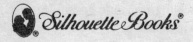

This April,
Silhouette *Special Edition* is pleased to present

ONCE IN A LIFETIME
by Ginna Gray

the long-awaited companion volume to her bestselling duo

Fools Rush In (#416)
Where Angels Fear (#468)

Ever since spitfire Erin Blaine and her angelic twin sister Elise stirred up double trouble and entangled their long-suffering brother David in some sticky hide-and-seek scenarios, readers clamored to hear more about dashing, debonair David himself.

Now that time has come, as straitlaced Abigail Stewart manages to invade the secrecy shrouding sardonic David Blaine's bachelor boat—and creates the kind of salty, saucy, swashbuckling romantic adventure that comes along only once in a lifetime!

**Even if you missed the earlier novels,
you won't want to miss**

ONCE IN A LIFETIME #661

Available this April, only in Silhouette *Special Edition*.   OL-1

SILHOUETTE'S "BIG WIN"
SWEEPSTAKES RULES & REGULATIONS
NO PURCHASE NECESSARY TO ENTER OR RECEIVE A PRIZE

1. To enter the Sweepstakes and join the Reader Service, scratch off the metallic strips on all your BIG WIN tickets #1-#6. This will reveal the potential values for each Sweepstakes entry number, the number of free book(s) you will receive and your free bonus gift as part of our Reader Service. If you do not wish to take advantage of our Reader Service but wish to enter the Sweepstakes only, scratch off the metallic strips on your BIG WIN tickets #1-#4. Return your entire sheet of tickets intact. Incomplete and/or inaccurate entries are ineligible for that section or sections of prizes. Torstar Corp. and its affiliates are not responsible for mutilated or unreadable entries or inadvertent printing errors. Mechanically reproduced entries are null and void.

2. Whether you take advantage of this offer or not, on or about April 30, 1992, at the offices of Marden-Kane Inc., Lake Success, NY, your Sweepstakes numbers will be compared against the list of winning numbers generated at random by the computer. However, prizes will only be awarded to individuals who have entered the Sweepstakes. In the event that all prizes are not claimed, a random drawing will be held from all qualified entries received from March 30, 1990 to March 31, 1992, to award all unclaimed prizes. All cash prizes (Grand to Sixth), will be mailed to the winners and are payable by check in U.S. funds. Seventh prize will be shipped to winners via third-class mail. These prizes are in addition to any free, surprise or mystery gifts that might be offered. Versions of this Sweepstakes with different prizes of approximate equal value may appear at retail outlets or in other mailings by Torstar Corp. and its affiliates.

3. The following prizes are awarded in this sweepstakes: ★ Grand Prize (1) $1,000,000; First Prize (1) $25,000; Second Prize (1) $10,000; Third Prize (5) $5,000; Fourth Prize (10) $1,000; Fifth Prize (100) $250; Sixth Prize (2,500) $10; ★ ★ Seventh Prize (6,000) $12.95 ARV.

   ★ This presentation offers a Grand Prize of a $1,000,000 annuity. Winner will receive $33,333.33 a year for 30 years with interest totalling $1,000,000.

   ★ ★ Seventh Prize: A fully illustrated hardcover book published by Torstar Corp. Approximate Retail Value of the book is $12.95.

   Entrants may cancel the Reader Service at anytime without cost or obligation to buy (see details in center insert card).

4. This Sweepstakes is being conducted under the supervision of an independent judging organization. By entering this Sweepstakes, each entrant accepts and agrees to be bound by these rules and the decisions of the judges, which shall be final and binding. Odds of winning in the random drawing are dependent upon the total number of entries received. Taxes, if any, are the sole responsibility of the winners. Prizes are nontransferable. All entries must be received at the address printed on the reply card and must be postmarked no later than 12:00 MIDNIGHT on March 31, 1992. The drawing for all unclaimed Sweepstakes prizes will take place on May 30, 1992, at 12:00 NOON, at the offices of Marden-Kane, Inc., Lake Success, New York.

5. This offer is open to residents of the U.S., the United Kingdom, France and Canada, 18 years or older, except employees and their immediate family members of Torstar Corp., its affiliates, subsidiaries, and all the other agencies, entities and persons connected with the use, marketing or conduct of this Sweepstakes. All Federal, State, Provincial and local laws apply. Void wherever prohibited or restricted by law. Any litigation within the Province of Quebec respecting the conduct and awarding of a prize in this publicity contest must be submitted to the Régie des Loteries et Courses du Québec.

6. Winners will be notified by mail and may be required to execute an affidavit of eligibility and release, which must be returned within 14 days after notification or an alternate winner will be selected. Canadian winners will be required to correctly answer an arithmetical skill-testing question administered by mail, which must be returned within a limited time. Winners consent to the use of their names, photographs and/or likenesses for advertising and publicity in conjunction with this and similar promotions without additional compensation. For a list of our major prize winners, send a stamped, self-addressed ENVELOPE to: WINNERS LIST, c/o Marden-Kane Inc., P.O. Box 701, SAYREVILLE, NJ 08871. Requests for Winners Lists will be fulfilled after the May 30, 1992 drawing date.

If Sweepstakes entry form is missing, please print your name and address on a 3" x 5" piece of plain paper and send to:

In the U.S.
Silhouette's "BIG WIN" Sweepstakes
3010 Walden Ave.
P.O. Box 1867
Buffalo, NY 14269-1867

In Canada
Silhouette's "BIG WIN" Sweepstakes
P.O. Box 609
Fort Erie, Ontario
L2A 5X3

Offer limited to one per household.
© 1991 Harlequin Enterprises Limited Printed in the U.S.A.

LTY-S391D

SILHOUETTE·INTIMATE·MOMENTS®

NORA ROBERTS
Night Shadow

People all over the city of Urbana were asking, Who was that masked man?

Assistant district attorney Deborah O'Roarke was the first to learn his secret identity . . . and her life would never be the same.

The stories of the lives and loves of the O'Roarke sisters began in January 1991 with NIGHT SHIFT, Silhouette Intimate Moments #365. And if you want to know more about Deborah and the man behind the mask, look for NIGHT SHADOW, Silhouette Intimate Moments #373.

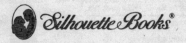 *Silhouette Books*®